The Wheel and the Day

The Wheel and the Day

Michael Cabrera

REBEL SATORI PRESS
New Orleans

Library of Congress Cataloging-in-Publication Data available

1

I met June at Nationals Park, embedded in a congregation of Christian evangelicals. Samuel and Benny sandwiched between us in their Sunday best grins, hiding their held hands beneath a big brown blanket while religious folks cheered across the baseball stadium. It was the middle of May and the Washington, D.C. weather was uncommonly cool.

A stage flexed between second base and the pitcher's mound. Giant banners rippled "Capitol Crusade." The T in "Capitol" was a crucifix. The screen below the scoreboard flashed with images of the crowd—some in tears with their hands in the air.

"We love Jesus, yes we do," one side of the stadium screamed. "We love Jesus, how about you!" The other side repeated. We sat dead center in front of home plate with no idea as to which side we were supposed to be on. Samuel and I finally decided to join the left while Benny and June screamed as the right, a perfect representation of the District.

The music interrupted the wave. Sam and Benny didn't participate. They wanted to sit snuggly behind their blanket and hide their affection. It was just June and I, our hands in the air. I caught sight of her smile and I thought, *well, hello there June.* Her bouncing brown eyes responded back and we spent the last two waves staring only at each other, two people in a sea of thousands, waving at each other until the music started.

We were met with electric guitar chords and banging percussion. I could tell the band was trying to give off a hard rock feel, but Christian rock always has this wholesome sound to it that undermines the edge of secular rock.

After the music died down a middle aged man stepped onto the stage wearing a Hawaiian shirt. He was our evangelical speaker for the evening. He went on about his life story: selfish hedonism to selfless devotion. Folks cheered and "ahhed." At the end, as was expected, he gave a chance for us to step onto the field and "have what he had," to accept Jesus in to our hearts.

"We're going to play a song for you now," he said. He swayed a bit as the guitar strummed softly a tune that I recalled from my days in church as a kid. I felt immediately uncomfortable. Samuel had his eyes closed in prayer, but I could tell he was peeking at me now and then. I'm sure Benny was giving June the same treatment.

"If you want to accept Jesus Christ as your Lord and Savior, step right up here and open your hearts to him." The speaker waved a hand in the air. "Don't let your pride get in the way. If you have to, grab a friend. They'll be happy to walk with you."

Samuel had his eyes open and stared at the stage monstrosity with dedicated fervor. I knew he was just waiting for me to ask him. Benny was less passive. He turned to June and said, "If you want me to go with you, I will."

She had a side smirk. Her short brown hair swept her eyebrows as she looked at me and said in a fake southern accent, "Why Jacob, would you be so kind as to escort a lady to the altar to say her prayers." I couldn't hold back the smile.

Across the stadium, people cheered the "new believers" picking their way down steep concrete steps to the field of ushers waiting with new believer packets. I stood up and motioned for June to lead the way to the center steps. The folks around us cheered; no one louder than Sam or Benny. I squeezed my way in front of the two gay men, my ass end in their faces.

"Now don't get excited," I said to them. Samuel slapped my leg and Benny laughed. June and I walked arm-in-arm to the center stage, the world around us in an uproar, singing our praises. She rested her head on my shoulder.

On the field, we were lead into a prayer confessing we were sinners, accepting the death and resurrection of Jesus on our behalf, and asking the Holy Spirit to enter our bodies. I won't pretend I felt nothing. I've said this prayer several times in my life, all times of loss or difficulty, after feeling I've wandered too far from my upbringing or when I needed to feel a connection to what was home in my mind. I always felt warmth when I said these words, regardless of sincerity. It didn't feel like home, anymore. It felt like someone else's home and I was just looking into the window smelling their supper.

A woman greeted us after the prayer. She introduced herself as a counselor and then went into what she believed Christ had done for her. "I was a prostitute," she started. June's smile faded slightly into concern.

"No, no," the counselor, said. "My past is my past and I am now a saved and new person by the blood of Jesus, just as you are now." She handed us New Testament Bible's and a few booklets. One was titled, "Questions Critics Ask."

The original plan after the "spiritual gathering with a good message," as Samuel had described it to me when he invited me that morning (I should have known 'a good message' was code), we were to meet at the Johnny's 24-hour Diner for food. Johnny's was a tired looking restaurant with brown carpet and a musky scent. Benny was tired and Samuel actually had to work the next day. So, June and I went together.

Johnny's had a few from the crusade there. Some of them had their new believer Bibles stacked in the center. Most were laughing and smiling.

June and I sat in a booth near a window facing the Metro station across the street. A yellow lamp hovered above us dressed in a retro style steel rim. A mini jukebox played "Crimson and Clover." She ordered a salad and I picked at chili fries.

"So are you really religious?" She asked me. She flicked a cherry tomato to the side of her plate.

"Me? Not really. You?"

She shook her head. "Benny seemed anxious for my soul. I felt like I should just indulge him."

"Yeah, Sam was giving me the side-eye treatment."

"I'm glad you came down with me." She smiled; her brown eyes softened in the warm light. Everything about her was beautiful: from her waving chestnut hair to her light brown skin. She wore a baby blue blouse and slacks, and I looked underdressed compared to her in my black tee shirt and khaki cargo pants.

I had just inhaled some fries and covered my mouth. "I swear I'm smiling back at you. It's not pretty though."

She laughed.

"So what brought you to the D.C. area? Benny tells me you're originally from California."

I swallowed my food and sipped some water. "Military. I was stationed near here and just stuck around. You? Are you from around here?"

She shook her head, "I'm from Florida. Miami area. I came here for work. What branch?"

"Navy. I was a Corpsman. It's like a medic but they ship us out with Marines sometimes."

"Yes, I know. My father was a Navy Corpsman. Did you deploy?"

I nodded, "Afghanistan. One year. No military for you?"

"No, I went to school and now I work for the government. Lots of paperwork."

"I'll bet."

"So, what do you believe, if you don't mind me asking?"

"That's a good question. I don't know anymore. You?"

She shrugged. "Spiritual, I guess. Not really religious."

"What does that even mean?" I hoped I could get away with some mild teasing.

She smiled, "It means I don't like organized religions, but who am I to say there's nothing up there, you know?"

"You mean, like in space?"

She raised an eyebrow and smirked. I got the feeling I was pushing it with that one. I raised my palms in surrender. "Fair enough. Fair enough," I said.

"Look at us talking about religion on the first date," she said naturally, without a hint of awkwardness.

We took the Metro together afterward. It wasn't too late and the trains were on extended weekend hours. We both lived across the river in Virginia. She asked me a few more questions, mostly about the war and I asked her for her number and she wrote it on the inside of a gum wrapper.

We officially dated after that. We thanked Samuel and Benny profusely for introducing us to each other, but when they asked if we would ever come to church with them we politely declined. We figured we were okay with the Christian God despite this since, after all, it was Jesus who brought us together.

June eventually moved in with me in an apartment complex off the Pentagon City Metro stop. It was a two bedroom sitting on top of the Pentagon shopping mall. For a while it was bliss. Then, it was love and the love was good.

It wasn't until a year later in the month of June, June's favorite month as it turns out, we headed on a camping trip to Seneca Rocks, West Virginia. We invited Benny and Samuel with us. Neither were much for camping. Benny wanted to rent a cabin. Samuel seemed willing if just a little reluctant.

We took separate cars up the winding back roads and climbed forested dirt trails to our spot with a view of rocky cliffs and bright green foliage. There was a stream nearby for fishing and swimming and some caves for guided tours.

The summer was especially hot and humid that year and we spent the noon hours hiding in the shade and whining for evening, eating sweaty peanut butter sandwiches.

There were only a handful of other campers. Most had massive tents and giant tarps strung up for shade. June and I felt especially terrible for Benny, who was sunburned, worn out, and the most vocally miserable of all of us.

"Maybe we can go to a hotel, nearby?" Benny said from under a huge pair of white sunglasses.

"We couldn't afford it," I said, "but if you two want to take off…"

"We're fine," Samuel waved. "Benny likes to whine. If we were in a hotel, he'd complain that there weren't enough hot guys in the pool."

Benny scoffed at this. "I thought there would be hot guys here. Instead all we have to look at are the old fat guys with their shirts off."

June walked passed me and grabbed a water from the ice chest and I pulled her to my lap.

"Stop it. You're too hot!" She pushed her way up.

"Thank you."

June slapped my chest and I heard Samuel laugh.

Benny shook his head, "Ugh, straight people."

"And we have you too thank, my friend," June ran her cold water bottle over her neck. I resisted the urge to pull her to me again.

Benny chuckled, "No, honey, that wasn't me. That was definitely Jesus."

We swam at the water hole when the sun wasn't so direct. It was cool and clear but the tiny fish bothered Benny and the restrooms were covered in spiders and smelled like rot. There was a cave a few miles away that sounded like a nice idea. We set out in Samuel's car with our wet feet wrapped in towels.

June and Benny sat in the back and chatted away about their college days and Samuel and I chatted about the military. There was a chaplain we both knew. She was short and wiry. She used to visit our outpost in the Western region of Afghanistan. No one went to her chapel services, but we all joined her for cigars in the evening while evening prayers played over the loudspeaker in the Afghan village outside.

"What do you think?" Samuel asked me.

"About what? The Chaplain?"

"No. About the evening prayers."

I hesitated, not wanting to disrespect Samuel's interest in religions but also wanting to be truthful. I gave up and shook my head. "I thought it was creepy, Sam," I laughed.

Samuel nodded his head and smiled, "I did too."

"Really, you? I thought you were big on their dedication to faith."

"I respected it. But I didn't like it. When a religion goes mainstream it's like it loses its original meaning. It becomes shallow and everyone claims to be it because that's what they're used to."

I faced Samuel. He wasn't smiling at all.

"Mainstreaming, huh?" I was going to make a hipster joke but Sam's unwavering face made me reconsider.

"Yes, mainstreaming. It means the religion has to cater to everyone, including fools. It contorts itself to fit ignorance instead of staying true to its original message of spirituality." He heaved a sigh and I noticed he gripped the steering wheel tightly.

"Are you okay, man? What happened?"

Benny chimed in from the backseat, "Our pastor won't marry us."

"That's awful. She seemed so open to you two." June said.

Benny reached up and squeezed Samuel on the shoulder, "She said her conscience just wouldn't let her. We were against her teaching."

"What the fuck?" I started.

Samuel nodded, "I know. I get angry thinking about her."

"No, that's not what I'm talking about. You were going to get married and not tell me!" I punched him on the shoulder.

"It's called an elopement. We wanted to run away together."

"It's actually because he's afraid of his future Mother-in-law." Benny chided.

I shrugged my shoulders, "Now, that I understand. You should meet my potential Mother-in-law."

June flicked my ear.

At the cave tourist trap, we filed into a large log-cabin style gift shop and bought tickets. We had an hour to kill before the next tour and Benny and June checked out the sunglasses.

I sidled up with Samuel at the arcade games, shooting poorly rendered deer. I was always the better shot than Samuel. This was sad considering he was the gunner and I was the medic on our deployment.

"Go ahead and say it," he said, holstering his yellow plastic rifle into the cheap black pouch. I had clearly beat him.

"I win? You're a terrible shot?"

"Not that. About the pastor. Let it out."

I sighed, "Why are you Christian if they don't accept you for who you are? I mean, why bother?"

"It's where my heart is," he said. "It's what makes me who I am."

"Bible thumping makes you who you are?"

He threw me a glare and I knew I went too far. "Fuck the Bible. It's not about the Bible. I have spirituality. I feel the presence of something bigger than myself when I immerse myself in my faith. I love it. I'll never push it on anyone. I mean share it with folks, maybe."

I knew he was talking about the time at the crusade, which he apologized for profusely. "Evangelical crusade aside, no, you haven't pushed anything on me. I understand you. But why can't you find your spirituality somewhere else. Why a Christian church? Why not anywhere else?"

"Like I said, it's a part of me. It's a big deal to Benny too. I was raised on that style. I shouldn't have to be ashamed of that because the religion has been abused in the past or people can't understand the main message and run off on single-verse tangents over what you shouldn't do. I like it."

"Okay, I get it. I'm really sorry." I leaned up against the coin machine. I could see Benny and June heading toward us. Benny was pointing at his watch. Samuel started walking toward them.

"Hey," I said, "If you and Benny get married... I mean, if you find a good pastor in a more progressive Christian church or something, don't leave me out of it. I want to be there."

He nodded slowly and we all walked to the cave entrance together.

June held my hand during the entire tour, not letting go even when the guide invited us to touch the underground waterfall.

"What if I trip and get sucked down some cavernous hole?" She kept saying.

"That's what the rails are for."

"What if the rail becomes loose?" She squeezed my hand tighter as she mentioned it.

The guide, a pretty blonde in safari style clothing, described the formations and made jokes about the shapes. There were a few kids on the tour and, though they didn't find the jokes as funny, their parents laughed cheaply. I eyed the layers of rock and wondered how much was above us and nervously imagined it all falling down on us.

Then, I thought about what Samuel said about his faith. I was raised Christian too. My mother, a devout woman with a less-than devout husband, would drag us every Sunday and every Bible study in between. It was pounded into me, screamed at me, guilted into me. To me, I could only see manipulation and fear, but Samuel saw something else. He saw hope. I wondered what that was like.

When we reached the farthest part of the tour, the guide shut off the lights and allowed us to experience the deep echo of absolute dark. I was surprised that even the kids were quiet. June rested her head on my shoulder and we held each other, man and woman, in infinite black. In the void.

What is out there? In the back of my mind I thought of Samuel's words, "something bigger than myself."

I thought of some great Spirit experiencing the darkness I was.

Let there be light? Maybe. Maybe not. *If you're out there. I want to know you.*

We weren't supposed to be drinking alcohol at our campsite, but considering everyone else had bottles of wine and the camp grounds security didn't seem to care, Benny opened up his secret stash he had stowed away in a small ice chest in his car. June and I were on cooking duty that evening. We had a few hotdogs burning on forks with soggy buns ready on paper plates. We each got pretty tipsy. We sat in a circle around the fire and told stories and laughed as the sun burned bright orange between the cliffs in the distance.

A few clouds whispered in from behind the mountains looking like balls of foam rolling across the sky.

"Beautiful," I said in a drunken stupor. "Don't they look beautiful?"

June reached for her glass and sipped quietly, watching the clouds roll in and cover the entire sky. The orange light simmered to dull gray and a chill ran across the grounds. No one said a word until we saw the black mass seeping over the mountain peaks.

"That doesn't look good," Benny said. "Actually, that looks quite terrible."

Across the park, people gathered their things, quickly dumping them in boxes. We watched them, still slightly intoxicated but aware enough to follow suit. June gathered the food and hid it into the ice box. Benny and Samuel helped toss many of our supplies into our tent.

The winds picked up to a whistle. Leaves, dust, and a few lightweight wrappers from campers far away sailed across the sky above us. The black mass consumed the grey in the sky and we were enclosed beneath a blanket of darkness.

Rain pelted our faces as what we hadn't moved in time scattered across our site. Tarps from other campers tossed wildly from their cords and sailed upward to join a sudden explosion of lighting above.

I shouted to Benny and Samuel to get to their tent, my voice lost in the wind but Samuel understood and led Benny away. June, clothes matted to her body, struggled with zippers as our tent bowed in the wind. After doing a quick sweep of our area, tossing our drenched chairs under the picnic table, I joined June in our tent, catching a glimpse a trees bending over and hoping nothing fell on us.

It was humid and hot and June and I dressed down to our underwear as the tent walls danced wildly and the lightning strobed silhouettes of trees.

"What is this?" She screamed at me. I could barely hear her.

"I don't know. I've never experienced this before."

Leaks sprung inside and I pulled a tarp and twine out from one of our duffle bags and ran outside in just my shorts. The tarp twisted madly as I tied corner after corner. I had a flashlight but didn't need it. The lightening was continuous and intense. I finished the final corner before finally looking up at the sky.

My fear was tremendous but the sight was too breathtaking to tear away from. I could see level upon level of swirling cloud cover as lighting jumped from tuft to tuft, sometimes exploding in a firework and dancing magnetically into the blackness. Debris skimmed across the sky in an almost tranquil stream, like dark angels in formation.

I stood in horizontal rain, my heart pounding in my chest, my breath escaping me, while something tremendous tore across my world.

"Something bigger than myself," Samuel had said.

I stood amazed and nearly naked in mud, facing this force of wind and water and electric blue fire. "Is that You?" I said to it. "Did you answer my prayer? Are you calling me?"

"What are you doing, you idiot!" June screamed at me from inside the tent. "Get inside with me!"

"Babe," I hollered back, thunder rolling with my voice, "it's beautiful! Come out with me."

She carefully picked her way into the mud and stood by my

side. Hands held, we watched the lightning display, felt the tremor of thunder in our bellies, licked the rain from our lips, breathed the air of the chaos around us.

"It's beautiful," I heard her say.

We held each other until, just as quickly as it had arrived, the storm trailed off into the distance, taking its lightning with it. The rain settled to thick fat drops from the trees around us while the wind sighed to a soft cool breeze. The clouds separated and we witnessed the multitude of stars. The moon appeared then, and we could see the rest of the campsite around us, in disarray. The fireflies came out and mimicked the lightning that had just taunted them moments ago.

June checked in on Samuel and Benny while I gazed at the moon. I could feel its pull, strange as it sounds. I could feel the stillness of the earth beneath me and the endless expanse of the sky above me.

"How beautiful You are," I whispered.

In my heart I heard a whisper back, "As are you."

2

Carmen was over. I hated her.

Throughout my military career I ran into a lot of strong women. I never had a problem. Strong women were direct. They screamed when you did something stupid, and didn't scream when you were doing what you were supposed to do. I can handle that. June is wrong when she says I can't handle her mother because I can't handle her "strength." Bullshit. Carmen was a passive aggressive demon, unapologetically disapproving, traditionally demeaning, and selfishly intrusive.

"So, you're still unemployed?" She picked at her Eggs Benedict, not looking up at me. "I hear you spend all day at home."

"How do you like your eggs?" June asked. She had on her light blue silk nightgown.

Carmen, the short devil, wore her dead pink robe hiding her heavy body. Her hair was tied back in a net. She was in a more pungent mood than usual, even for her.

"I'm *self*-employed, Carmen." I responded. I made sure I was showered and dressed, shoes on, a gym bag packed, all ready for an outburst and a walk-out.

"You would think you have to actually work to be considered employed," she said, sucking in egg-yolk like a creature from a horror film.

"Mom…" June started.

I interrupted, "I'm having a slow period, Carmen. At June's request, I took time off to enjoy your visit. How long are you here again?"

"Jake," June shook her head.

Carmen didn't seem affected. "What is it you do again?"

"Massage therapist."

"Oh, is that so! I see lots of women giving massages at salons," she turned to June, still avoiding even looking at my direction. "Margie is a massage therapist, June. You remember Margie?"

"Yes, mother, I do," June sighed.

Carmen smiled, her teeth peeked past her lower lip. "Of course you do. She's the one that got married to Sergio."

June rubbed her temples.

"Ah, Sergio," Carmen continued. "He was such a handsome man—a manly man." She flexed her arms sending her pink robe in rolls over her chubby arms. "I thought for sure it would be you who would get married to Sergio. But anyway."

She tore into her egg, letting the yolk run down the English muffin.

"By the way," she inhaled half of her food and chewed wildly, sending egg bits across her plate, "I opened that chest you have in there. I found all those very strange books."

I was about to say something but June raised a finger. Even June had a limit to how much she could take from her mother. "What were you doing in Jake's things?"

"I was looking for an extra blanket," Carmen said flatly.

"They're in the closet where I told you," I snapped.

"These books were so strange. I think they were about Satan worship! It scared me. I saw pictures of evil things!"

"Are you sure you didn't find a mirror?"

"Jacob!" June's eyes widened on me. She and I had an agreement. She would be the one to confront her mother, not me. I was too ...*much*. June turned to her Mother who was feigning hurt. "Jacob is researching *paganism*, Mother, not Satanism. You had no right to go through his things."

I hated it when June took over. It made it sound like I was five.

"So you feel you are above Christianity now, you have to go and

14

make up your own religion. You know it's all made up, don't you?"

"How do you like the eggs, Mother," June interrupted.

Carmen smiled at her, "They're delicious sweetheart. I've taught you to be a great cook."

June smiled back, "Thank you, Mother. Jake actually made them."

Carmen scooted back is if she just found out the eggs was poisoned. Her face was a mixture disgust and horror. I could tell she was working out a clever explanation for her previous comment.

"You can save it, Carmen." I said as I reached for my gym bag on the couch. "I'm not going to argue with you."

"You'd lose!" She snorted.

I heard them arguing as I stepped away from the apartment and to the elevator. There were small children outside so I had to hold in my anger and look somewhat friendly and approachable. With fists clenched I stepped into the Pentagon City area, walking a few yards before texting June, "Let me know when it's dead or asleep." I was sure to hear about it later, but there was no point in pretending to get along with June's mother.

I pictured her fat body slugging around the apartment I paid rent in, mocking my life and dismissing my military service as "boys with toy guns" compared to what her husband accomplished, god rest his soul. She milked her husband's death every chance she had. I'm sure she was doing it now to push away any apology.

I made it to my gym and lifted weights my body would regret. Every clank of cold iron was a spike of hate I imagined into Carmen's blubbering body. Every curl was a punch in the gut to every coward who didn't have the balls to handle what I did in the military. *People. They like running their mouths.*

Thoughts that could have put me in a nut house ran through my mind as I worked my routine. I wondered how Samuel dealt with it. He and I never talked about the angry effects of the war and how it seemed to triple negative emotions, but then again, whenever we talked, we wanted to remember our camaraderie, not the disturbing aftermath.

I could feel the emotions mixing with the adrenaline and suddenly I was in a better mood. I finished off with a treadmill run and headphones screaming in my ears to drown out the gym pop music.

After a shower, I left the gym. My body steamed slightly in the cool morning air. I knew I didn't want to head home right away so I locked my gym bag in my car in the garage and took the yellow Metro line to DC. The yellow line had the best view of the Mall from the bridge that spanned over the Potomac and dived again into the underground. The skyline of the domed memorials with, what I always called the 'national erection,' the Washington Memorial, set tourists on a camera happy run to the windows.

I got off near the Mall at the Archives station. D.C. looks immaculate near the monuments. The brilliant marble with the high level of security, it almost reminds me of some patriotic section of Disneyland.

The Smithsonian museums were packed. It was a Saturday and a pleasantly temperate Saturday at that. Kids and strollers crammed the sidewalks with half-interested parents pacing lazily. I struggled against the crowd. I went to the Jefferson first since it was a little harder to get to than the others.

The Jefferson memorial has this cathedral-like echo inside. There are signs posted, telling you to keep your voice down, but kids can't read. I kept my distance and faced Jefferson who looked slightly pissed off from where I was, hands at his side and tight lipped.

I stumbled around the tidal basin walk with cherry blossom-less tree branches slapping my face as I dodged tourists. I avoided the Washington Monument and World War II memorial, and stopped by the reflection pool long enough to hear someone comment about the bird shit caked on the sides. After a quick glance at the crowd near the Lincoln, I decided to wander to the park behind the White House and watch the birds or something.

I was still frustrated by Carmen and her "pleasant" stay with us but that seemed more distant after my workout. The thought of her and June deciding to take a calming trip to see the monuments didn't hit me until I was seated near one of the statues. The rage was back.

I won't blame my anxious temper on the war. I will say that I had a better handle on it before my deployment. It was the storm inside of me that magnified the little annoyances excused by most ordinary folks. It was blinding and suffocating. I felt so powerless and tied up. I knew I was starting to manifest these thoughts externally. I was getting looks across the park and so I stepped up and started walking around some more.

I didn't want to be that guy anymore. I didn't want to feel so helpless and frustrated. I thought of June and what she meant to me. I tried to keep my thoughts away from Carmen who triggered this enraged reaction with her… self.

I trickled away from the tourist cloud and walked onto diagonal streets of D.C., homeless people on every corner, squatting near buildings dressed in marble. I dropped a few dollars into the violin case of a man weeping my tune. *Always happy to help an artist.*

"You don't have any more than that?" He said while stroking his strings.

I ignored him and stepped out from under an awning and let the sun hit my face.

I made it to the park at the end of the road and realized I had walked part of the pentagram that was said to have been strategically placed with the White House at its peak. I wondered how much of that was true. I didn't feel any special lines of energy surging through me. No special waves of magic hitting my soul.

I caught sight of a group of kids wearing the same colored t-shirts, maybe a school field trip. I decided I had enough of D.C. for one Saturday and I headed to the nearest Metro station and trekked away from the city and into Alexandria, Virginia's King Street Metro.

Alexandria is one of my favorite places to wander in the D.C. Metro area. It has the cobblestone streets, the uneven sidewalks, and even the colonial style buildings, but only a fraction of the tourists.

I stepped out into the summer air with the late afternoon sun still blaring against pointed roofs. Someone played the saxophone somewhere on a street corner. There was a trolley bell dinging up and down King Street. I wandered into an African antique shop and admired some of the carved wooden statues with their wide grins. The gentleman behind the counter followed me around the aisle and pretended to rummage through some boxes. I left.

I found a new age bookstore, just halfway toward the riverside pier. A smell of incense wafted from inside. I peeked around, for some reason feeling vulnerable. When I felt like no one I knew was walking around a corner (God forbid, Carmen) I stepped inside.

The inside smelled like nag champa incense with notes of cedar. It was arranged with a few bookshelves in front and various stones, herbs, statues, and other spiritual oddities in the back. I stood just a foot in front of the doorway and soaked in the scene.

My first thought was, *Wow, there are a lot of people in here.* I wondered how many of them were just like me, having wandered into the shop as outsiders. But I caught a pentagram necklace here, an onyx bracelet there, a couple tigers eye rings, and it hit me that they were all regulars. Regular looking people in a very irregular themed shop. I froze, feeling exposed. I ordered all my books online or in the miniscule new age section at the major bookstores. I never actually been inside a new age shop.

"May I help you, sir?" said a short man with gray hair and beard. He stood near the register with a brunette who had on glasses.

"No, I'm fine. Just browsing," I managed to say after a stammer. I pulled myself away from the door and glanced at the first set of books I could find.

Astrology.

I never liked the subject. Something about the planets and stars telling someone what their personality is going to be made me roll my eyes. But maybe there was more to it? I pulled out a book and glanced through some charts.

Time flew by while there in the shop. I had rummaged through all the topics, catching authors and titles to memory. I didn't want to buy more than I could handle. I did have a great deal of books back at the apartment.

I thought about the apartment and wondered if Carmen and June were still back there. I groaned quietly into a book about magical protection. I heard someone shuffle nearby and I turned to a late 20-something with red hair wearing black glasses. He mulled over some book about spirit guides.

"Interesting stuff, huh?" I said suddenly. It was awkward but I had a reason.

The guy hardly looked up. He just nodded and said, "yeah."

"You know any groups that practice stuff like this? Like covens or anything?"

I heard him snort. "I don't know. Have you tried online?"

"Online! Yes, of course. Thanks." I shelved the book I was holding and headed out the door. I didn't look back.

The apartment was empty when I returned home. There was a note on the fridge: "Took Mom to Baltimore for the weekend. Tried texting but you didn't answer. Love you, June." On the counter rested a plate of cookies I'm sure June made.

I picked up the plate to find another note: "Mom made these." I tossed them in the trash.

I pulled my laptop from the desk in the living room and plopped down on the couch. There were a few webpages there about paganism but I was having horrible luck finding active groups. The ones that were active weren't meeting until some holiday in August I couldn't pronounce, spelled "Lughnasadh." I sent out a few emails to the group organizers, hoping I would get an immediate response from someone, anyone, but that was asking too much.

On a local discussion board, I typed out a call for any pagans in the area. Impatiently, I watched my email well until the sun began to set in my apartment windows sending stripes of black and orange into the room from behind the blinds.

Frustrated, I shut my computer and went into my guest room, Carmen's stuff was gone. I pulled out my books and tools from the chest Carmen had invaded earlier. I had a knife, called an athame (pronounced ath-Ah-may), a metal cup I bought from a random craft shop—a chalice, and a short stick I had whittled—my wand. I felt foolish holding these items in my hand. They felt like toys, but maybe that's all they were. Maybe I was wasting my time.

A book on Wicca was tucked underneath a few candles. I pulled it out and skimmed to the part about tool dedication. There was mention about doing some things completely in the nude, or skyclad, but I didn't know how comfortable I felt about that. The book mentioned that usually tool dedication was done by another Wiccan on behalf of the newly practicing individual, but I wasn't having much luck finding anyone thus far. The next best thing, the book said, was using one's own body or hands to dedicate the tools. I actually felt that was a lot more appropriate than having some random stranger touching my tools.

I folded the guest futon and got to work setting things up. There were lots of candles to be placed. I didn't have many color candles, but I did have various tea light holders. I placed a green one in North for Earth, a yellow in East for Air, a red in South for Fire, and a blue in West for Water. With one hand holding up the page in the book with a picture of an altar, I did my best to organize a table tray as close the picture as possible. Then, I happened to glance at the bottom of the picture that read, "one possible option."

Interesting…

I wondered how much flexibility this stuff had. What if I wanted to change some things up? After all, I didn't really want to leave the rigid Christianity of my youth for another rigid system. I had a bowl of salt, some incense, as well as my wand, athame, and chalice on the small altar. I had two jar candles marked for the goddess and god according to the book, but that felt uncomfortable right now.

I took the god and goddess candles off and left one large white pillar candle to represent that experience I had in the mountains during that storm. The memory was still so fresh in my mind and I could feel a strange tug on my heart when I thought of it. If there was a god or goddess I believed in, it was whatever that was, for now.

There was a moment where I only stared at the altar in front of me and reflected on what I was doing. How weird was it, a grown man, in his 30's, an allegedly grounded war veteran, standing in the middle of the room with what would be considered toys to most other folks? I felt strange and yet, I felt somehow freed from the opinion of others considering that this is what I wanted to do. I craved this. I craved more than what any other religion could give me.

I took in a deep breath and, without much thought, I kicked off my clothes and tossed them in a corner. Completely naked, I felt a little more connected and yet a lot more exposed. If there was a god or goddess out there, watching me doing this, what were they thinking?

They probably wouldn't care if I dressed in a loincloth and feathers.

I concentrated on my body for a while. I imagined my soul within my shell becoming large and enveloping my body with a glow. Then, after some deep breathing, I imagined my mind, a sea of random thoughts calming in the wind so I could concentrate more. Then I pictured a connection, the part of me that was higher than I was and yet a part of me, haloing above my head. The part of me that could connect with divine. I breathed in the air around me and let that part of me glow brighter and brighter until I felt it completely covered me. When I felt calmed, I traced a circle around me with my finger, starting and ending in the East. I imagined it flickering in blue flames. I could feel them.

Each direction was honored and called with a raised hand. And finally the Divine, I called with my outstretched arms as I did in Pentecostal church.

"If you're out there, if what I experienced was real, let me feel you in this circle."

There was a still presence that circled me. I felt warm and cold, full and empty at the same time. It was the type of ecstatic experience I could never give to anyone or describe fully. I felt both deep joy and sadness.

Using the salt, the incense, some water and the flame of the candle, I consecrated my tools for use in the magic arts. It felt good but it didn't feel like enough. So, I laid them all out in front of me and closed my eyes, imagining blue flames shooting forth from my hands and into my tools, cleansing them, strengthening them, blessing them, and empowering them.

Time stood still as I did this. Or did it? I felt like I was swimming in time; I swam in between realms of the Universe. I was in the room but I wasn't. I was somewhere enchanted and beyond the physical. I could feel my body but my body was somewhere else. I could touch my tools without moving my hand.

The sensation was exciting and alarming so I opened my eyes. It was dark now except for the candle burning on my altar and the tea lights dying down around me. There were other lights too, small ones, like the fireflies echoing the lightning of that storm. They hovered as I rubbed my eyes.

Then, they faded out of sight.

"Was that real?" I asked out loud. I was a bit nervous I would hear an audible voice respond back at me. I met with only silence.

It was just in my head. Just in my head. All of it. In my head.

3

Matt was the first person who contacted me. He responded to the discussion board posting and I agreed to meet with him at his place for a conversation. It was a few days closer to Lughnasadh (I found was pronounced "Lew-nassa") but I was getting impatient. None of the other pagan leaders in the area responded to my emails.

Matt's place smelled of stale cigarettes and cat litter. It held towered boxes and newspapers.

"Ignore the look of the place," he said. "My roommate who owns the place is a bit of a packrat."

Matt himself stood slightly taller than me, but not by much. He was an older gentleman with square glasses. He wore a white T-shirt and loose shorts. It was warm in his home, which made the cat litter scent nauseating.

We chatted about where we came from. Unsurprising, he moved to DC from the Midwest with dreams of getting into some kind of political lobbying. I hate talking about politics so I asked him about the upcoming pagan holiday.

"It's the celebration of the death of the god figure. It depends on who you ask really. The god sacrifices himself for the harvest, that sort of thing," Matt said.

"A god sacrificing himself, eh? Reminds me of Christianity."

Matt's face turned sour. "This is older than Christianity, thank you. Christianity stole that idea from pagans!"

I nodded, "I see."

He showed me his ritual space, as he called it. I guessed my ritual space would have been my guest room. He had an open altar in his bedroom. It was a lot more fantasy inspired than mine was. He had a dragon holding a stick of incense which he lit while I watched. There were various stones and a few stone orbs of quartz on tiny pewter bases. I asked him what he did with them.

"I scry every now and then. I don't really need them though. I do have *the sight.*" He told me.

"Can I pick them up?"

"Sure. Go ahead."

I lifted a stone orb he said was obsidian. I allowed the weight to shift in my hand as it rolled across my fingers.

"Do you feel its energy?" Matt asked me.

I shrugged, "maybe."

"Well, you'll be able to in time."

Maybe.

"So," I asked, "What is 'the sight?'"

Matt pondered this while I flipped through his book shelf. There was a book about men in Wicca and what their role was. The more I read about Wicca, the more it seemed to dichotomize male and female almost against each other.

"The sight is a gift," Matt started, "some witches have it and some don't. It lets you see things that many people can't see, like auras, fairies, sometimes the future."

"Fairies, eh?"

Matt nodded. "Not the Victorian kind that look like pretty skinny folks with wings. Fairies vary greatly in appearance. Some are terrible beings capable of murder. Some are bashful and keep away from you. It really depends on your energy and if they're drawn to you or not."

"Interesting…" I would have to delve deeper into the topic of fairies and see what they meant to me, if anything.

I thanked Matt for meeting with me. He asked me to stop by again soon, and, though I said I would, I never did.

At home, June seemed less than pleased at me visiting some

strange man at his home.

"What if he knocked you out?" She said. She was tossing a salad, which I would normally make a joke about but she seemed in far too serious a mood.

"Honey, nothing happened. I wasn't knocked out."

"But he could have!"

"And what? Sacrificed me to Satan?"

"Who knows? Or raped you or…"

I scoffed and she threw me a hard stare.

"Okay," I said. "Okay…." I trailed behind her and kissed her lightly on her neck. I loved her neckline. It was slender and slightly browned with her Latin American skin. "…no more meeting strange men in their homes, okay?"

She shrugged me off and plated the salad with some golden chicken she had sliced earlier. We ate in the dining area and chatted about our days. Massages weren't terribly busy but I was getting by. June worked in marketing and she found herself busier than usual.

"You should quit," I told her.

"And go where? I need a plan if I'm going to quit."

"Just live at home with me and I'll take care of you."

June laughed and I admit, I was a little hurt by it. "I'm sorry, honey, but you don't make all that much for that."

I didn't. I should have expected that response.

I smiled and we ate silently for a while. She cleared her plate and started the sink, "Benny called yesterday."

"Oh, yeah? We didn't scare those two off with our camping storm massacre?"

June ignored me, "He wants us to visit him end of next month for dinner."

"Next month? Why the long notice?" I joined her by the sink and rinsed my dish. She dried her delicate hands on a dish towel.

"You know they're traveling in France."

"France, this time? They're always traveling," I said. Then I winced. I knew it was coming. She was still standing next to me with her hands already dried but wrapped nervously in the dish towel.

"They make decent money," she said and then she hesitated with only the sound of running sink water. I shut the faucet off and heard the echo of the drain. "Benny also said that they're hiring at Sam's work in government."

I felt an icy chill run up my spine. My heart felt gripped tight. There was sweat and it was cold.

"You know I can't...

"...It's been some time since your last, you know, breakdown, and I was thinking...."

"I still have them. I'm trying to get a hold of it but I'm not there yet..."

"If you get a good job we can take vacations like Sam and Benny and maybe that will help..."

"Honey, please..."

"Please, just think about it. Massage isn't working out like you'd hoped and we aren't doing that great."

I could feel the walls of the room closing in on me. I backed away from her abruptly and she attempted to get close. I raised a hand out.

"Stop," I said. I was breathing heavily. "I can't."

"Okay," she whispered and she backed away from me. "But you need some help for this. We can't live like this forever. I support you helping yourself, but we're going to need more eventually."

I watched her walk away to the hallway and into the bedroom. Explosions were running in my mind. I grabbed my keys and left the apartment.

There was a time when Samuel and I talked about this problem frequently. When we got back from the war, we made it a habit to meet at a local dive nearby and talk about our deployment team. It was dark and quiet and we had to speak in hushed tones.

"Are you doing okay?" I would ask him. He actually had it worse than I did.

Samuel would nod his head slowly and he would talk, sometimes for hours and I would listen and ask him questions when it felt right or I would just keep my eyes glued to his and be as attentive as I could even if I was hurting as much as he was—this is what brothers in arms did for each other when the bullets stopped flying and the explosions weren't loud enough to shake one's teeth. We listened. Sometimes I was the one who talked. Either way, we were there for each other and I loved Samuel because of it.

We met once a week at first, spilling our guts and complaining about civilian life, but then it gradually tapered to once a month. Soon our conversations were less about our issues with life after the war and more about how well things were going. Samuel was the first to crack the emotional block. He said it was Jesus who did it for him.

"I'm not going to push my faith on you," he told me, "but I want you to know that it worked for me. Maybe it'll work for you too."

I would nod, but deep inside I was shrieking away. I had my Christian days already. I didn't want them anymore.

Samuel must have sensed this because he added, "I don't care what faith you choose, but I recommend finding something to believe in. Something. It helps to believe in something. I promise."

We stopped these meetings after that. It didn't feel right to push my misery on him. Though, there were times when I could have used them. There were times when the instinct to cut and run was so fierce, so detrimental to other jobs I've held, I almost gave in and called him.

Now, my best friend was in France and I was alone walking the streets of Arlington, Virginia after dusk, unsure where to go. It felt so congested outside: the cars, the buildings, the crowds of people. I wandered to a park nearby and sat in the center of a large sports field. There were trees, but not enough to block out the incessant noise of the city. Not enough to darken the lights so I could see the stars again.

I closed my eyes and imagined the great Divine being, whoever it was, behind the brightness, calling down to me. I pictured that stormy night clearing, when the clouds tumbled away and all that was left were those fireflies echoing the lightning in the trees and the millions of stars twinkling. I imagined them speaking to me, healing me, filling me with their essence.

"Fear not the dark," I said out loud, "For without the night sky, how would we see the stars?" I don't know where I got it from, but it felt right and I smiled. "If you're out there Great Spirit, Goddess, God, whatever you're called. I need you."

The sounds of the city had died down to some distant rustling that could have been a spring of water for all I knew. There was silence after all of that. Not a sound or voice. I only heard my breathing in the dark. Maybe that was the sign.

When I opened my eyes I realized I had cried. Embarrassed that some onlooker may have seen me, I wiped my tears quickly with the sleeve of my light jacket and then checked my phone.

There was a new email from one of the groups I had contacted, "We would love to meet you and see if you're interested in our Druid group. We're having a Lughnasadh celebration next week. You are welcome to join us." It was signed "Blessings, Peter and Nasaide." There were directions and time located in the email. Excited I stood up and walked back to the apartment.

The next week was painful. Lughnasadh fell on a Wednesday and the celebration was to be held the weekend before. I had that to be thankful for at least.

Luckily for my wallet, massages were in high demand that week. This helped with my impatience as well, though I didn't feel like I gave my best with each client. No one complained and many complimented me, so I had that to be thankful for.

June remained quiet about me finding a new job when she saw how much I had made.

"Maybe this will work out after all," she said and she kissed me on the cheek.

"Hey," I started. I met her eyes. "Please be patient with me. I'm getting over it all; it just takes more time for some of us."

Then Saturday finally arrived and I rode into the deeper parts of Virginia just outside the DC metropolitan area. The house sat on a cul-de-sac in a porch lit area, heavily wooded. I could smell the damp scent of a lake somewhere nearby. Cars lined up and down the street with pagan stickers and a few rainbow flags and Obama stickers. I wondered how political pagans were.

This group was a Druid group. It wasn't high on my list of groups I wanted to associate with, but at this point any group would do. Besides, there was a part of me that figured that the group would be mixed with general pagans and maybe, hopefully, other fellow curious individuals like myself. I didn't want to be alone.

I heard the laughter and music on the other side of the front door. The door itself was dressed in a wreath with a twig pentagram resting in center. I knocked and waited. Nothing.

I felt cold sweat on my brow and suddenly I realized I was about to have a panic attack. I was so nervous. My breathing, labored and short, my vision blurring. I stepped back and was about to run to the car when I heard the door open.

"I thought I heard someone." A warm female voice called out. "We're not in ritual."

"Excuse me?" I turned and faced her.

The woman stood roughly my height with long burnt auburn hair that shone like fire with the house lights behind her. Soft skin and light colored lips on her freckled face, she was thin except for her belly which protruded out, pregnant. She had one hand over it, resting softly on a summer white dress.

"We haven't started yet. You can come in if you'd like." She didn't lose the warmth in her voice.

"I see," I said, suddenly not feeling anxious but stunned. "I'm Jake Ayers." I extended a hand.

She shook it, "Nasaide." She pronounced it "Nah-say-dee."

She continued, "Come on in."

I stepped in, catching a glimpse of fireflies in the bushes outside.

I was greeted immediately by a man wearing plaid shorts and grey T-shirt.

He shook my hand, "You must be the new one that emailed us. I'm Peter."

"Ah, it's great to meet you."

"Likewise," he smiled.

They lead me through a hallway lit by candle-like sconces and into a wooden-themed living space where the other pagans congregated. My heart raced in my chest.

"Everyone," Nasaide said, and she motioned in my direction, "this is Jake."

I was introduced around the room. There were so many people I had a hard time keeping track. I did reacquaint myself with a few, though.

There was Sophia, a heavy older woman with curly brown hair. "Welcome to the community," she said. "Have you experienced many groups yet?"

"No," I told her. "This is actually my first."

"A solitary?"

"A what?"

"How long have you been practicing? Have you been practicing a while and just decided to come out into the community?"

"No," I said, "I'm brand new. I just started..." I thought a moment about the one ritual I performed at my altar. Would she understand if I explained "consecration of tools?" Did Druids do that kind of thing? "I just started with all of this less than a month ago."

"Oh, wow. You're very new. Very new." She rubbed her chin and tilted her head slightly. "There is someone I should introduce you to very quick."

She took my hand and lead me through tufts of conversations. When we stopped I stood before an elderly woman with wild gray hair, wearing a draping gray tunic, and sitting in a large armchair.

"Lenore," Sophia called.

Lenore looked up at her, "Oh, Sophia. I promise I'll make the next gathering…."

"Oh, Lenore," Sophia waved her hand. "I'm not here about that." She motioned to me, "This is Jacob. He's very new to paganism, less than a month, he says."

I smiled at her, "Hello."

Lenore looked up at me, her face was wrinkled and absent of make-up. She let her mouth hang open in a smudged 'o.' She looked remarkably wild. If I had seen her in the street, I would assume she was homeless.

"Why hello, Jacob," she said. She took my hand into her right and blanketed it with her left. I felt her warm old skin on mine.

"It's nice to meet you, Lenore."

"Indeed, you as well."

Sophia pitched in, "Lenore is an elder in our community. She runs the Green Man Tribe, a group here in Virginia."

"We have members from all over," Lenore said. "Maryland, the Capital, but many are here in Virginia. If you're interested, you are welcome to join us there too."

"That sounds great," I said. "I was hoping I'd run into a variety of pagans here. Druidry seems interesting too, but I'm not sure where I'm going to go just yet."

"Oh, honey, take your time," Lenore said. "And don't worry if something isn't for you. No one gets offended."

"At least they shouldn't," Sophia interjected.

Lenore continued, "We all have different paths. I practiced Druidry here with Peter and Nasaide, but I have my own tradition I am apart of as well. Keep in mind, you don't have to choose just one, either. Be careful of anyone that tells you otherwise. They like to control you, those types."

"I see," I started.

"Are you solitary?" Sophia asked again. When I showed signs

of confusion, she asked, "Are there others you practice with?"

"No. I don't know anyone else. I've only been doing this a month," I said.

"Well!" Lenore said, "Welcome to a new world, indeed!" She laughed in an old cackle. Lenore was every bit what I would imagine was a faery tale witch, only without the evil intentions. She continued, "May I ask you what brought you to this new path?"

"I've always been curious about paganism," I started. "I was never really active with it until that storm came by a couple months ago."

"Aw, yes," she nodded. "Powerful energy in that storm."

"I know. I was camping when it hit," I explained.

Sophia gasped and Lenore gripped my arm dramatically.

"Camping in that storm," Lenore shook her head. "I'll bet you experienced the raw power of Earth Mother in that storm."

"Yes," I said. "I felt something, that's for sure."

Lenore asked me to join her group around what she called "Samhain" (pronounced sow-en). "The ritual will be somber in the theme of the Sabbat, but we have a great celebration afterward." She prodded my side with a light elbow. "We like to have fun in our group. None of this 'oh-too-serious' stuff."

I thanked her and walked the party a bit more.

A few more guests arrived in the already crowded living area. In the kitchen, Nasaide pulled out a roast from the oven and Peter turned some potato skins on a grill skillet. I offered to help but Nasaide assured me they were fine.

I spent a lot of time sipping water and eyeing the crowd. Many were middle age. A couple were in their twenties while a few more were in their early thirties like me. It made me feel less awkward. I half expected to walk into a house of goths.

One young man brooded slightly next to Sophia who seemed to be having a solemn discussion with him. I recognized him almost immediately as the young man I ran into at the new age shop in Alexandria: my height, skinny, red hair with dark eyes. I nodded at him and he only half smiled back.

As the roast cooled in the kitchen, Nasaide called us all to the front parlor room with a fireplace. A table sat in the center with a most items I recognized. A large central candle pointed up from the center with a bowl of water, a stick of sage, some incense, and a bowl of salt. I knew they represented the four elements, but I was unfamiliar with Celtic deities to guess who the statuettes represented.

"That's Brigid and the other is Cernunnos," the young man whispered to me. He stood next to me behind the sage stick which was apparently sitting on the table corner pointing south.

"How can you tell?" I whispered.

"Brigid is goddess of the forge, see right there?"

That female statuette was indeed striking an anvil. The male figure was horned and appeared to be holding up a bracelet of some sort and either a snake or a hookah pipe.

He continued, "the forge is a huge symbol in paganism, and Cernunnos is a pretty popular image for Druids. See, he's holding a torc and a snake."

"I'm Jacob," I said.

"Corey."

"It's nice to meet you."

"So what did you think?" Peter asked me. We stood outside on the deck looking into a dark tree line.

I smiled and nodded my head, still feeling the rush of adrenaline, the tingling of residual butterflies. I was so nervous during the ritual. *Are we going to sacrifice an animal? Are we going to summon the devil?* For a much hyped pagan ritual, I was surprised with how tame yet fulfilling the experience was.

"Feel good about it?" Peter asked again.

"Yes. I feel…" I took a deep breath, "refreshed. Even grounded."

"I'm glad." He took out a cigarette and we talked about our experiences.

Peter was traveling for work when he decided to pursue paganism. His family was torn by it. His first wife left him for another man, his children, though supportive, distanced themselves from his new path.

"I'm sorry to hear that," I said.

"Don't be," he flicked ash into a small cup on the deck railing. "It changed my life for the better. I have Nasaide now and the kids, well, they're not kids anymore. They eventually came around."

"So why paganism? Why did you decide to go this route?"

He took a deep breath. The folks inside the house were cheering and laughing. I caught a glimpse of Corey watching us from inside.

Peter started, "Well, there is one main religion in the country and I can't say I did well in it."

"I hear you there."

"Paganism, it's what you want it to be. You can make it shallow and destructive, or you can make it deep or uplifting. That's the beauty of it. You have no one to blame but yourself. There's so much to it too. There are so many avenues you can take, so many ways to flavor it that you can't do with mainstream religion," he shook his head.

I let him continue, "That's not it either. That's only part of it. When I think of my spirituality I see it as connection with the earth, the sky, the trees, animals, other people, stars, planets, everything. It's overwhelming and yet so simple. ...I don't know if that made any sense to you or not, but there it is." He laughed.

I thought about that storm and looking up at an infinite sea of stars and feeling my name called by something, someone in the spaces between the little lights, and somehow in the earth I stood on, in the water dripping from the trees, in the fireflies twinkling with the distant lightning and thunder.

"Yes," I said. "That makes perfect sense.

He finished his cigarette, patted me on the back and left me alone with my thoughts. I joined the others only a short while later. The commotion had died down a bit after some left, carrying paper plates wrapped in aluminum.

"Now, no pressure," Sophia said before she left, "but I do have my own group, just a few friends of mine. I would love it if you joined us sometime."

4

My thoughts were on the ritual for the rest of the month. It was so simple. Nasaide traced a circle with her outstretched palm as she walked around the outside of the congregation. We all held hands and recited, from a script, a few prayers and lines of acknowledgement regarding the season and the lore of the harvest king giving his life for the harvest.

The lore felt outdated but the overall feel was what mattered and I felt a certain boost of excitement having honored a season. I was disappointed, however, at how there was no actual magic practiced at the ritual, but I suppose that wasn't the point of it. I still wanted to find a group that practiced what I considered to be an interaction with the forces of nature, but I was left with a ritual. A beautiful one, but still only a ritual. *Did pagans not practice magic during their sabbats, their main holidays?*

I pondered this as I worked the following week. Massage was its own ritual with me and that week I felt more in tune with it, the grounding, the gliding, the music and the motions. It's a dance to me. Every client that comes across my table is my dancing partner for 30, 60, or 90 minutes. I would never tell them that of course, but I knew they appreciated my work.

This week I visited Mr. Jameson in Rosslyn. He liked his neck and his back worked on. Mrs. Bolero was a piano teacher with pain in her hands and wrists.

No problem. Let me turn on my music and I'll glide with you. I'll dig into your muscles. I'll relax your nerves.

Each client had his own energy, and they were usually males, most wanting, sometimes demanding, a little extra at the end. I'm always the professional.

"I can't do that," I would say. "I can lose my license."

"You're kind of cute," they would tell me. "Just this once."

I won't lie. There is a sexual side to massage. Not that I see it as a purely sexual experience, but I am touching someone else's body. I am running my hands on curves and notches, over lines and soft spots that would be denied most people, but it's in the name of health. I have a level of trust I need to ensure in my clients, and I don't abuse that. I won't.

I won't abuse Collin, a twenty something who competes in bodybuilding competitions locally, or Sandra, who swims regularly and needs work on her rotator cuff muscles. They aren't my sexual partners, they're my dancing partners.

This is my ritual and it's one I do for the sake of health and money. I love my job, despite the feast or famine momentum it has. Despite the weirdos I get every now and then.

One gentleman had the audacity to call 15 minutes before his appointment and ask, "So should I have condoms ready or do you have some."

"Sir, I think you have the wrong idea of what goes on during a massage."

Kathleen calls on me for work on her calves. She's a runner and she suffers from night cramps. Mr. Hashim calls me because his wife died and he needs an escape. I hear him cry under my hands. I can feel the sadness near his heart through my hands.

"How much did you make today," June asked. She was washing dishes and I sneaked behind her and nibbled lightly on her neck. She smelled like lavender.

I told her the amount and a smile stretched across her face. It's going to be a good month for us. A few weeks go by and I wait patiently for the next pagan get together. A full moon ritual was scheduled on the night planned for dinner with Sam and Benny. I considered canceling dinner plans but I really wanted to see them.

Still, after the rush of a new pagan crowd, I was hungry for more.

I checked the social websites for local witch groups. There were two, an eclectic Wiccan group, called Inner Fire, that wasn't meeting until Samhain, and a closed female-only group. The eclectic group sounded alright, but I wanted something sooner than Halloween.

The week of the full moon I got a call from someone in the Druid group. It was Corey, the stand-offish guy with the brooding face.

"I hope you don't mind, I saw an ad out with your number for massage," he said.

"Oh, yes." I said, "I'm a massage therapist. Did you want one?"

"No, actually," he hesitated. "I wanted to see if you could meet for coffee. You seemed new to this pagan stuff. I figured you'd have questions."

"Ah," I was excited but the call felt somewhat date-like. Just to be safe I added, "well I'm booked today with clients and I'm making dinner for my girlfriend, June tonight. Maybe tomorrow?"

"Sure, that sounds great." He gave me his phone number and we hung up.

That night after dinner I wondered if I could get away with calling him. Maybe he would meet me at a bar or late-night restaurant for dessert. I was too excited. I thought better of it and decided just to do some meditation on my own. Maybe practice circle casting.

I kissed June on the forehead and said, "I'm going to do some stuff in the guest room."

"Oh? What kind of stuff?"

I staggered. "uh… some witch stuff?" I realized I had never done anything like this with June in the house. How would she react?

June dropped her jaw slightly and her eyes widened. "Oh." She looked around as if trying to find something to do. She started to clear the table.

"Don't worry about it, babe. I'll get it when I'm done. Shouldn't be long." I told her.

"I see," she said. She still held a plate in her hand. She straightened up and asked, "Do you mind if I watch some television while you do that?"

"Not at all, if you don't mind keeping it down a little."

"Sure."

And that was the end of it. I wondered what went on in her mind but I figured I'd never know for sure. She seemed okay with my new path.

After casting a circle, I decided to pull out a set of tarot cards and ask them what was going on in her head. I didn't exactly know how to read them. I would just go after the pictures and maybe whatever the book that came with the deck, said.

I asked, "What does June think of my new path?" I pulled the Ace of Wands: new beginning, fire, creativity. That didn't seem too bad. I shuffled the cards again and asked another question.

"What will this Corey guy bring me?" I pulled a Five of Wands. There was a picture of a group of guys holding staffs trying to hit each other with them. The book said "competition." I'm not a competitive individual by any means, so I figured this card was a fluke and I should continue meeting this guy, if just with a little caution.

After pulling the cards, I didn't know what to do. I sat in the circle and imagined myself back on the mountain with the storm ravaged campsite and the distant clouds rumbling and flashing… and all those stars. More than I could ever hope to count.

"Whatever you are," I said to the presence I felt, "Let me experience you more."

When I closed my eyes I thought I could feel those stars twinkling within my own body.

I met Corey at a coffee shop in the Pentagon Row area. Pentagon row sits near the shopping mall with a mirage of high rise style shops on the ground level. Apartments sit on top, including

June and my apartment. There is a patio that doubles as an ice rink when winter comes.

I found Corey outside the shop wearing jeans and a black polo shirt. It highlighted his pale skin.

"Let's go inside and grab coffee," he said.

"Okay."

He ordered some fancy latte and I ordered an Earl Grey. We didn't say much at first. He stared at me a while and tried to sip his coffee which was too hot. I knew my tea was too hot so I only watched people pass outside the giant double-paned windows.

"So what did you think of the ritual the other day?" he asked finally.

"I thought it was good. I'm new so there isn't much to compare it to, you know? I liked it though. The whole 'honoring nature' thing was pretty attractive to me."

I couldn't tell what his opinion was. He half smiled into his cup and said, "yeah, I guess that part was cool. They don't do much else though. The Druid group isn't big on practicing magic."

I felt my ears perk up. "You know magic?"

"Of course. I'm a witch. We actually do magic."

"How do you learn?"

"Someone shows you how. Practice."

I pondered this. *Who would I get to show me?* I was too new to the community to pick anyone and allowing someone to teach me was a bigger deal than just finding someone and going with it. A relationship had to be established. A rapport.

"Any other ways? I'm kind of new here to just trust anyone right now."

"Well, you won't find anyone around here that teaches much anyway. Just a bunch of flakes and white-lighters and you don't want to learn from them. They would hardly show you anything anyway."

"What's a white-lighter?"

"A fluffy bunny. A new age hippie that believes only in good white magic, and that harm-ye-none bullshit. Usually anyone that calls himself "Wiccan," but not all of them."

"I don't understand. Why would I want to harm anyone in the first place?"

Corey sighed. "You know what? Forget I said that. You're too new. You'll figure it out when you run into them."

I got annoyed when he said that. I wondered if the 5 of Wands, guys hitting each other with sticks, was right. Corey came off pretty condescending, but for now, he was the only person to talk to so I indulged him a bit.

"What kind of witch are you?"

"Hard to say. I'm not really a white or black witch."

I was going to ask him what that meant but he explained, "a black witch is one that practices only in retaliation or to get what they want. A white witch only practices what most would call 'good' magic: healing, protection, that sort of thing."

"Then how would you label yourself?"

"I don't. Let's go walk around, yeah?"

Outside, my hot tea felt foolish. It was humid and sunny that day. I wiped a few beads of sweat from my forehead with my forearm, still a little oily from massages earlier despite the number of hand-washings.

We decided strolling to the pentagon city shopping mall would be best and we headed to the sublevel entrance across the alleyway, just below the parking structure. The air conditioning was refreshing.

"A *real* witch is neither white nor black, good nor evil. A *real* witch is both because nature is both."

"That's from *The Craft*, isn't it? You're quoting things from *The Craft*."

Corey laughed at this, "it's still true." I laughed with him.

We both decided to toss what we had left of our hot drinks and go for frozen yogurt instead. We took the escalators up the glass covered eating area and made our way to the fourth level overlooking the shopping mall. A few birds caught inside the building flew by.

"Do you believe in god, Corey?" I asked him.

"No," is all he said about it.

We chatted a bit more about where each of us came from. I told him my story about the storm and he didn't respond much to it. He told me he was raised Christian and hated it. He found a boyfriend around the time he was 18 and able to leave his parent's house and they lived a happy pagan life together until they broke up a couple years ago.

"What are you doing these days?"

"I work non-profit. Doesn't pay well but it gets me by somewhat. I asked a few community members if they would let me stay with them but they all slapped me away."

I wondered if that was why he was so bitter about other pagans, or at least, that was how I perceived him.

He continued, "I live with Sophia now. That talkative woman you met at the party."

"She seemed kind. That's nice of her to take you in."

Corey shrugged his shoulders. "Yeah, I'm just a little bitter that is where I'm at right now. I just expected to be a little more self-sufficient you know?"

We wandered down a level and checked out an electronics store. Corey eyed a new computer while I checked out the cameras.

"So, where do you suggest I get training if not from anyone around here," I asked him when we met up again. It seemed we were headed for the exit and about to part ways.

Corey shrugged, "I don't know. Try online."

5

When I got back to the apartment I immediately went to the computer. There was a moment where I had no idea where to look. There was so much information on witchcraft online but there was nothing that was tangible. No real pictures. No classes mentioned. Nothing about distance learning. Most sites only had a philosophy about witchcraft or had very demeaning opinions about other groups and seemed very focused on how different they were from those 'other guys.'

Then I ran across a page, decorated in brilliant blues and purples. It took me a second to realize that it was peacock feathers I was looking at. The tradition was called Feri and I had no idea what it stood for. A few glances on the page and I realized it was a tradition a couple in California came up with. The story of the gentleman, Victor Anderson, had something to do with being initiated as a child by a woman. There was a lot of sex involved in it but I didn't mind it. Or did I? I continued to read through the website and found a list of teachers that taught both one-on-one and through a distance learning course. One of them really caught my attention.

The teacher's name was Justin Folly and he had a very artistic biography that interested me. "My art is created through my work in Feri," it read. I'm not such a creative or artistic person myself but I found that idea to be satisfying considering how much emotion seemed to be placed on my new spiritual path.

I read through the parts of the website that spoke about what the tradition believed it. For the most part, the group seemed pretty ecstatic. Personal and emotional experience dictated the tradition's flow. There wasn't much dogma sensed on the pages of sigils and pictures of gods and elemental spirits. Then I read about their main deity and my heart stopped.

The Star Goddess.

How beautiful it sounded. How true to my heart. I thought about the storm and the clearing that shown afterward and how it impacted me to see the stars, the dark between their settings, the moon and the way the whole world danced with me, in sync together, like my massages. We had danced in that moment.

"Yes," I said. "This is for me."

There is an application process that needed to be completed and mailed to the teacher for approval for the class. I let my cursor blink over the empty white pages of my essay, wondering if I was doing the right thing or if I was just rushing. This is, after all, the first group I was aware of. Weren't there other groups out there?

I decided to hold off on the application. I had a few more massages to do that day anyway.

The days rolled by and the time came for Samuel and Benny to return from their trip. I couldn't wait to see Samuel. I wasn't sure how he would take my new path if I were to tell him about it. I just felt happy.

They both wore matching polo shirts, at Benny's request of course. Benny, true to his sense of individuality, also wore a pair of teal pants with his while Samuel kept to standard dark jeans.

"Kisses for all," Benny said and he broke out in French I didn't understand.

"How was your trip?" June asked. Samuel handed her a bottle of champagne and a cheese wheel they brought back from their vacation.

"Oh you know, dear. Big crowds. Little time. Poor Sam spent a big deal of it sick," he said.

Samuel coughed, "food poisoning."

"The food wasn't poisoned. Sammy just has no stomach for foreign cuisine." Benny said.

It's true. Samuel used to get sick every time we ate Afghan food when we were deployed. I had to force him to stick to MRE's.

We talked about their trips to the Louvre, the museums, the countryside. Sam and Benny apparently had an eventful time. June had cooked a spinach lasagna and I had a rolled cake that I made for the occasion with a homemade whip cream topping. We were both proud of our cooking skills and we were pleased to see Samuel and Benny gobble them both up quickly.

We spent that evening at a bar within walking distance. It was a campy gay gathering but it had a fairly mixed crowd. It was a karaoke night and although none of us sang, Benny insisted June join him for a few songs from some musical neither she nor I had any knowledge of.

"Benny may be incredibly too cultured for us," I joked with Samuel.

"He's too cultured for me," he laughed.

We chatted about life and work. He was concerned I wasn't making enough.

"I do alright. I just don't do amazing."

"You think you can handle an office job, yet?"

I shook my head. "I freak out in small parties, I can barely handle massage clients…"

"But you're here now."

"It's different. You guys are here. June is here."

I nodded at June who was in the middle of singing.

"Plus I'm drinking," I added.

Samuel shook his head.

"I'm working on it. I really am. I just need to figure out how to turn off all that… noise," I said.

June and Benny finished. They got a giant applause from the drag queen MC, a curly-haired red-head named Cecilia. "I had to fan myself after that one," she said. The bar erupted in laughter.

45

Benny and June stumbled our direction. Both were drunker than I was. Samuel was sober.

He continued, "You ever wonder if it's a spiritual thing for you? Maybe you just need something to believe in to keep you going, you know? To help out with all that?"

Samuel never called it crazy; never called it panic attacks or mania or paranoia. It was just 'all that' when we talked about it.

"What are you two talking about?" June tripped into her seat and burst out laughing. Benny pantomimed swimming to his, the clown he was.

"Nothing," I said.

"Church stuff," Samuel said. He smiled at me.

"Oh, you're not inviting us to another 'special message' event, are you?" June rubbed her forehead.

Benny started laughing, "you mean like the one you two met at? How would that be bad? You two might leave married."

They both broke out in sobbing laughter that made me a little uncomfortable. I never know what kinds of things June talks to Benny about. I hoped our relationship wasn't one of them, but it was the most likely topic.

"Besides," June continued. "Jake here has wandered far from the Christian path."

"Oh did he now?" Benny said.

"Come on, June. Don't." I shook my head.

"Shhhhh," she hissed. "These are our friends."

"All friends here, Jake," Samuel smiled.

"All God's children," Benny laughed into his beer glass.

June sat up straight, looking like a news anchor about to deliver something exciting, "Jake is now a neo-pagan."

Samuel's smile faded slightly. His eyes looked stern which was muted somewhat by the flashing rainbow of colors coming from the stage. "Is that so?" he said.

I nodded, "I told you I was working on it."

Benny snorted, "All God's children."

The last karaoke singer left the stage. Cecelia, the drag queen, wished everyone a great rest of the night and opened the floor for dancing, introducing some young man in a tight white T-shirt as the DJ.

"Come on," Samuel reached out to Benny. "Let's dance."

Benny teetered off of his chair and chuckled. "Okay but you be careful with me. I'm delicate right now. You know what I mean!"

June started laughing.

"Come on and dance with me," she said to me.

I was never much of a dancer, but with her as drunk as she was it was easy to just hold her up and shake just a little bit. We danced later than we should have for a work night. A slow song finally came on and I let her rest her head on my shoulder.

"We should go after this," I whispered in her ear.

"Yes, but I have to tell you something," she whined.

"Okay, what?"

"I'm sorry."

"You're sorry?"

"Yeah, I'm sobering up and I just realized that I outed you about the paganism thing."

I chuckled, "nah don't worry about it. I'm kind of glad you did. They took it okay I think."

"I don't think most people care here in DC. In the South, they'd care."

"Yeah the South sucks."

"But not Florida."

"Especially Florida," I chided and I kissed her on the cheek.

"Jake?"

"Yes, honey?"

"I'm going to be sick."

She stepped away from me and rushed to the restrooms, nearly making it to the women's but making a sidestep right into the men's. Two guys ran out with looks of horror on their faces. I sighed.

The walk back to the apartment was a tumultuous affair. Samuel had to remind Benny what time it was. June straggled beside me. I could tell Samuel wanted to say something, and I was curious as to what, but he kept silent. They left us with the usual hugs and kisses. At home, June never made it to the bed. She snored quietly on the couch while I turned on the computer.

After a few minutes of reading over the Feri application, I typed up a response, printed it out and mailed it in the lobby downstairs. The Star Goddess seemed too perfect for me to pass up.

6

The second harvest festival passed without much going on. Mabon, usually the hallmark of Apple season, symbolizing either the goddess being found with child or the descent of Persephone, had no celebrations. Peter and Nasaide were out of town and the Green Man Tribe headed by Lenore was doing private group stuff being that it was the last of the Sabbats before the cold came in.

I decided I would do one on my own but wasn't sure how to structure it. The Druid group had a script with very descriptive writing. My style felt flat and uninspired.

"What are you doing, honey," June asked as I checked under the sink for tea light candles. I knew we had a few stored.

"Witch stuff," I said. I took to saying this whenever I felt the need to use the guest room and didn't want to be interrupted. Without much thought I asked her, "Do you want to join me?"

There was silence from the living room, where she was watching television. I heard a commercial running with the sounds of dogs barking.

"No thanks, dear." She said and I sighed in relief. I hoped I didn't make her uncomfortable. I wouldn't have known what to do if she had said, "yes."

After setting a tea light for each direction, I adorned my collapsible television tray altar with a small plate with sliced apples, one of those church jar candles for deity, whom I still had no idea about, and a few items I had prepared for a money spell. At the time massages were thin. People were on their last dash of vacation while the weather was still good. Many were government workers trying to use their 'use or lose' leave before October. I was hurting and June was making a bigger than normal stink about money. I figured what better way to celebrate a harvest Sabbat than with a money spell.

I performed my ritual. It didn't contain all of the elements I wanted it to, none of the fancy words that Peter and Nasaide used, but it did the job and I felt a great connection to it. Like my dance in massage, ritual is a dance with words and gestures. I made a few 'I honor the wheel of the year' statements to show the spirits, Elements, faeries, whatever, that I was paying my respects. A certain presence lingered in the room and I smudged with a sage stick when I was done because of it, hoping I didn't somehow open some doorway between hell and the guest room. That wouldn't go well at all.

My magic spell involved a green pouch, some five finger grass, a lodestone, moss agate, and a bit of abundance oil I gathered from an online shop.

Because of the type of spell I was casting I wasn't too worried about following the Wiccan rules of energy raising, the type of moon or the astrological signs in the sky. It was an anytime spell, but just in case, I made sure to at least time it around a harvest Sabbat. The energy, after all, was centered around reaping and collecting.

When I was done I put the anointed pouch in my pocket and took down my altar, making sure to take a few apple slices to the courtyard outside in honor of the spirits I worked with. I felt good doing this, and yet because I was alone, I constantly felt like I wasn't doing it right at all.

When I got back upstairs to the apartment I checked my phone and sure enough, it was packed with phone calls from new clients. I smiled big. My first spell and it worked perfectly.

Corey was one of those calls. I didn't respond because the last time we met he seemed to demean a lot of the people I had just met with his talk of 'fluffy bunnies' and his disdain for Wicca. I wasn't sure if I wanted to be Wiccan either but I would never talk down about it. It might not be my path, but that didn't give me or Corey the right to trash it. I would talk to him later when I was ready to deal with his attitude.

There was an email on my phone as well, from a Justin Folly. I recognized the name at once. The subject heading read, "Welcome to Feri."

"Can you hear me?" I asked.

Silence.

I fiddled with my laptop, the only computer in the apartment with a built-in webcam and microphone. The screen was choppy and blank for a bit and then suddenly brilliant white.

"Hello, Jake?" A voice said from my computer. I plugged my headset in and jumbled with the buttons on the keyboard. A few more clicks of the mouse and everything was fine.

"Hi Justin," I said.

"Oh, good. I was worried for a second. You never know how these things are going to work out."

I smiled at him and eyed the window that showed my own camera's feed. Making sure the angle was correct. I suddenly felt exposed.

In his own window, Justin Folly looked a bit older than his picture on the Feri website. He had greying dusty brown hair with a golden shimmer that shown clearly through his camera feed. He was heavy set with a slight bump under his chin. I watched him eye what I imagined was his own camera feed.

"Well," he said shuffling in his seat and adjusting the camera, "Welcome to Feri."

"Thanks."

"I sent you some exercises to start with. We're very big on daily practice and I want you to take your time with these. Really feel them. Let me first tell you a bit about myself, I am a Feri initiate— as you know we are an initiatory tradition, so there is only one degree. Completing this work is by no means a promise that you will become an initiate. Okay?"

"I understand."

Justin then told me about his spiritual path which was a mixture of what is considered Southern Conjure, a mixture of Irish, German and African magic that incorporated elements of protestant Christianity. He discovered Feri through a friend and was initiated into a line of Feri, and then joined his buddy's new line.

"From Victor and Cora Anderson, the founders of Feri, many initiates branched off and started their own lines of Feri with various flavors but a similar core," he explained. "Any questions so far?"

"Can you tell me about the Star Goddess you believe in?" I asked.

Justin sat back in his seat and smiled. "Right to it, eh?"

He continued, "Let me start by telling you a story. It's a version of our creation myth that I think you might like."

I leaned forward in my seat. I rested my eyes and pictured the story in brilliant vivid detail as he read from a sheet of paper in front of him.

"In the beginning, the Goddess was whole and complete. Her body was deep and black. She was and is the very void we see between the stars: the infinite space. Her body, at the time, hugged nothing but itself, swimming in a sea of darkness that was herself.

"As she moved, she felt her skin. Her own body reflected in the ebony mirror that is space. She became entranced with herself, with her reflection in the curved mirror: the voluptuous waves of her body. Feeling her body move upon itself, she became aroused: her leg upon her leg, her dark wings folded upon her sex. It was a dance with herself and with each step she blushed in brilliant blue. She writhed and quivered in lust until she could take it no more. She exploded in ecstasy. From a single spark of blue fire she spread out the many seas of stars that now dot the night sky, her own euphoric orgasm pushing energy outward, creating suns, moons, planets and heavenly bodies that tell her tale.

"As she reveled in the afterglow of her creation, she realized she was not alone. She had created another in her ecstasy. A youth with a blue body, blue like her dance; blue like sex. She loved him and he loved her. Together they danced across the stars, making love and loving their creations, spreading life among the tiny worlds they created together.

"…and that is our myth of creation," Justin said softly.

I had my eyes closed and felt myself slipping in and out of the present. I opened my eyes slowly, explosions of stars still taking place behind my eyelids.

"That was…" I stopped. Words couldn't describe it for me. Beautiful? Amazing? Yes, but it was more than that. It was my Goddess.

Justin and I talked more about what was expected of me while I remained of a student of his. I was to check in once a week on the same day and give him a detailed account of how my daily practice was going. We were to have an hour video chat at least once a month, and I thought that sounded reasonable.

After our video introduction, I immediately went into my guest room and set up my altar. I had a black jar candle ready for my first practice. After a quick wick trim, I set it in the center of the room on my wooden folding stand and shut off the lights.

I closed my eyes and concentrated on that storm, on the opening of the clouds, the twinkling of a billion stars. I lit the candle and began the prayer:

"Holy Mother, in you we live, move, and have our being. From you all things emerge and unto you all things return."

I stood in reverent silence, feeling the energy of the Star Goddess filling the room, feeling her dark body touch me, sending blue flames into me.

7

I wanted to celebrate but there was no one to celebrate with. I didn't feel I knew the Druids, Peter or Nasaide very well. Lenore was still a mystery to me. Sophia, though a fine individual, would have made for some awkward silences and staring into space.

"June, baby," I called to the living room. She was watching some cooking show where a British chef showed some restaurant owners how to run their business.

"Hrmmm?" She sounded from underneath a nest a throw rugs and pillows.

"Would you want to go out tonight, babe?"

The tassels of rugs and pillows swayed. Like some kind of mush monster rising from a swamp, June stretched and poked her head up from behind a pillow. "Not tonight, dear. I'm too lazy."

"Yeah, okay." I said. I reached from my hoodie draped over the back the arm chair near her.

"I love you, though," she whispered as I planted a kiss on her forehead.

As I reached the elevator in the outside hallway, my phone began to buzz in my pocket. It was Corey. I shrugged my shoulders and answered.

We met at a pub in Georgetown. Like anything in Georgetown it was overcrowded and teaming with obnoxious yuppies and pretentious college students. I didn't like the type but Corey seemed to enjoy admiring the men.

"So, you went with Feri, huh?" He asked. He sipped on a blonde in a pilsner while I gulped a microbrew of the red variety. It had a fiery and nutty aftertaste.

I licked my lips. "I did. It's great so far. I love the exercises they've given me."

"What'd they give you?"

I shrugged, wondering if I was supposed to keep it a secret. "Some grounding exercises and meditation techniques to practice. You know—the basics."

"Ah. That's good. A lot of folks don't have that meditation stuff down at all. They can't even sit still. It's good they're starting you off on that."

I sensed a slight condescending air about the way he said that, but dismissed it. It was hard to tell if he was being sarcastic or not.

He must have sensed it because he suddenly said, "I'm serious. I'm not being a jerk about it."

"Ah, okay." I took a final gulp of my beer and ordered another.

"Listen," he said as my new beer arrived. "I'm sorry if I came off crass last time we met. I wasn't trying to insult anyone, I'm going through some things with some of the folks in the community. I'd rather not get into it but I may have vented it out on you. Rotten first impression, I'm sure."

I was feeling buzzed and happy so I clapped him on the back, which is something I only do when I've been drinking, and told him, "It's okay, my friend. No harm done."

After another few beers we set out along the roads and just walked. I had taken the Metro to Rosslyn but the weather was still nice and I didn't want to go home just yet. We talked about home life. Corey was tragically single, while I was with the love of my life. I told him about how I wanted to marry June but money needed to be more of a sure thing.

"Why not find another job?" he asked.

I hesitated. "I can't handle one."

"Okay, I never heard that before."

I laughed. I was still feeling nice and toasted from beer. "I'm serious. I'm okay right now, right this second, but I freak out. I can't breathe. I get claustrophobic. My heart rate skyrockets. I nearly pass out"

"Sounds like anxiety."

"Maybe"

"Have you had it all of your life?"

"No. I deployed…"

"I see."

I kicked a small pebble off the sidewalk. "I don't tell many people about this."

Corey didn't say anything.

Wanting to change the subject, I said, "So tell me about magic."

"What do you want to know?"

"Is it real? Does it actually work when you cast spells and things?"

"You want to know if magic works and you already committed to a tradition?"

I shrugged. "That sounds like me."

Corey shook his head. It was hard to tell if he still felt buzzed or not.

"Yes," he said, "magic is very real. As a matter of fact, be careful with it if you don't believe in it. It's not something to just play with."

"So I'm supposed to fear it?"

"No. No. You're supposed to respect it." He paused, "Have you cast any spells?"

"Oh, yes." I said. "No curses or anything like that, if that's what you're asking. Just stuff to help me out when I need it. I did a prosperity spell last month for Mabon."

"And?"

"I got more clients, I suppose. I got paid and made rent. But it's hard to tell if that was the spell or just a really favorable coincidence."

"Magic works along the path of least resistance." Corey said flatly.

"Meaning?"

"Meaning if it's easier to give you clients for money than it is to have you win the lottery, magic is going to help you by giving you clients."

I sighed, "Well that's a buzz kill."

"Why is that?"

"I was hoping to be able to shoot fireballs out of my hands one day and from what you just told me, the only magic I'll be given is how to use a Molotov cocktail since, you know, that's easier."

I waited for a laugh from Corey, anything, but I could see that he was thinking.

"So you don't believe in the possibility of the supernatural portion of magic."

"I don't know if I do. I mean, can *you* shoot fireballs out of your hand?" I laughed.

"How about ghosts?"

"What about them?"

"Do you believe in them"

I shuddered. "Maybe. They could just be a figment of imaginations."

Corey didn't look pleased at me saying this. "Follow me. We're headed into the District."

"Where are we going?"

"Ever been in a haunted house?"

Yes, I thought, but I didn't tell him.

We wandered into the darker residential regions of Washington, DC. I nearly kicked a rat once or twice, but I stepped on plenty of roaches. I was asked a few times for money by homeless folks and I almost stopped for one, but Corey pulled me forward and we continued until my buzz was gone and the temperature dropped enough to make me wish I had brought a jacket.

"We're here." He said.

There was nothing too out of the ordinary about it. It was a white house that stood separated from the long lines of red brick townhouses that walled the streets. It had its own yard, small but enclosed in wrought iron fencing. It had its own driveway which is also unusual for the area. From what I could see there was a small garage out back as well.

"Nice house," I said.

Corey chuckled. "It's haunted." He pointed at the "for Rent" sign and tilted his head down, probably trying to look very grave. "A guy killed himself in there. The owners don't even want to live in there so the try to rent it out, only, no one will take it because the loon who killed himself still haunts the place."

He walked up a flight of concrete steps to the house's miniature garden area and then fiddled with a big box that was locked onto one of the iron fence posts.

On the sidewalk, I looked around before heading up. "What are you doing?"

"It's a lockbox. You put in the combination and it opens and gives you the key."

"Are we supposed to…" I started.

Corey cut me off, his pale skin illuminated by a flickering street light. "I know the real estate agent. He's a friend of mine. It's okay, trust me."

I shrugged my shoulders, but followed him to the front door where he put the key in. Corey pushed the door slowly allowing it to creak among the empty darkness inside. I stepped in first, catching the scent of old wood and paint. Corey followed and shut the door behind us.

"Feel anything?" he asked.

"I feel like we've broken in."

Corey sighed, "We didn't break in. Nothing is broken. I know the real estate agent."

As my eyes adjusted I caught site of a small lamp stand near the door, the only piece of furniture that I could see. On it, were brochures and some business cards set by Corey's "friend." We stood in a hallway that looked into the kitchen. I could see the appliances lit in faint blue, probably from a stove or microwave clock. Rather than open with a bannister, the stairs to the second floor were sandwiched between two walls. A window somewhere along the staircase dressed the steps in pale yellow light that flickered.

"Feel anything?" Corey asked again.

I shuddered. "Maybe. I mean, it is an empty house. Vacant houses are automatically spooky, right?"

The living room had hardwood floors like the rest of the place. The wooden planks creaked under me. I closed my eyes and tried to feel for something, not knowing what it would feel like exactly or if I was even capable of feeling it. Nothing.

"Sorry, Corey," I said, "I don't feel a thing in here."

He scowled. "Maybe you're too new and not as attuned as I am."

I felt a tinge of frustration at his words, but I kept quiet.

He shifted on moaning boards, his face a pale haze in the street lights coming in through the large front windows. His glasses gave off a shimmer.

"Let's go upstairs," he said abruptly and we headed for the enclosed stairwell. A window from high up the walls allowed us enough light to pick our steps, first, to a square landing, then to the second set of steps turned 90 degrees to the second floor.

We reached the top, a narrow hall leading to open doors and pale rooms on either end. The was one closed door in the center that Corey motioned to. He reached for the brass knob and turned. I heard the knob slipping under his palm and the sudden catch and click was loud enough to startle me. Maybe I was more nervous than I was letting on. Corey let the door creak open, for effect I'm sure.

"Step on in," he said. He motioned into the room which I could see from the tiling and the astringent smell of cleaners, must have been the bathroom. It was dark, though—too dark to see farther than an arm's length inside.

I reached for my phone in my pocket and flicked on the option to turn on my flash as a flashlight.

"What are you? A Wimp?" Corey started.

"Sure," I said. "A wimp that doesn't like to trip over stuff."

An old tub and shower set squeezed between the two walls at the end of the bathroom. An old but clean toilet sat near the sink. The mirror made me nervous if only because of old tales about Bloody Mary and I half expected her to be looking back at me on the other side. I shut off my phone flashlight.

Corey stepped in and shut the door, allowing the darkness to envelope us both. There was silence.

"Well…" I said.

"Shhh," Corey hissed from somewhere near the sink. "Concentrate. Sense anything?"

I sighed, then reached out with as much feeling as I could. Nothing. I could only focus on Corey and his abnormal breathing. Maybe if I were alone I'd be able to catch something. But if I were alone I wouldn't be in this house.

Suddenly, an image of a man entered my mind. His face contorted. Jagged teeth reached out from decayed gums and pulled lips. Rotten eyes.

No.

I shook the image from my mind. It's just my imagination.

"It's getting cold in here," I said.

"Notice where it's coming from?" Corey responded.

It was obvious it was from the tub. It was like touching ice when I waved my hand in that direction.

"Stephen Cook," Corey started, "abusive father and husband, lost his entire family in a drunken car crash. Feeling pain and regret, he moved here where he spent his days pushing everyone away until one day he couldn't take it anymore and murdered himself in that tub right there."

I stepped away from the tub. Another flash of a man cutting into his arm and weeping, ran across my mind. I felt his sadness. I shook it off. *It's not real. Just my imagination.*

"How did he do it?" I asked.

"He slit his wrists. They didn't find his body until he was a mess."

"Yes. I'm sure." I said. But the images I was seeing in my head, they were so obvious. Of course it was a suicide, why else would Corey have brought me into the restroom. Of course he was alone. Of course no one found him until… well… until his mouth receded and his gums had rotted. The images in my mind… it was just my brain connecting the dots.

"Well I've had enough of being locked in the bathroom. You ready to leave?" I said.

Corey huffed and I imagined his face was tight with disappointment. The door opened and the air felt free and less stale. We left the door open as we trampled down to the first floor.

"Well. I hope you felt something," Corey said sounding disappointed.

I shrugged. "I might have. It's hard to tell. This stuff isn't as obvious as I thought it was."

Suddenly a loud thump sounded from somewhere upstairs as if something heavy and limp where plopped onto the floor.

"What on earth…" I started.

"That was from the bathroom," Corey said.

Another thump, this time cleaner, like something getting up off the ground. Then, something took a step onto the hallway's hardwood floors.

"This is a joke, right?" I turned to Corey who was wide mouthed and open eyed, shaking his head slowly.

It's him. It's old man Cook.

There was another set of thumps that shook the ground, and then the unmistakable sound of a footstep on the stairs.

It can't be him.

Another step, and then a rustle of steps, and then a thump against the walls of the square landing.

But it is him.

"We need to go!" I shouted at Corey, who was still shaking his head in disbelief.

From the other side of the staircase wall, someone sighed, or maybe coughed. I pulled Corey forward and we scampered past the front door. I felt the cold chill of knowing that Mr. Cook was probably staring right at me as I ran in front of the staircase, just several steps away.

Corey shut the door and locked only top padlock. We scrambled to the lock box still on the wrought iron fence.

"I can't take the key!" Corey said nervously as he fumbled with the combination on the box to drop the key inside. I could hear the click of the front door handle. It, whatever it was, was at the front door trying to come outside and join us.

I forced myself to take one last glance at the door and I could see a figure looking back at me from behind one of the small rectangular glass panels on the door. I nearly tripped on myself as I sped down the steps. Corey and I ran passed the rats and roaches along broken sidewalk. I looked back once but saw nothing.

Just a squatter or some homeless guy who followed us in. It can't be Cook. It can't be.

8

I woke up the next morning around seven. June had left for an early company meeting, so I was alone in the apartment with rain pattering at the window. Stephen Cook wasn't in my dreams but he was in my thoughts and the memory of the house scared me enough to shut the restroom door before bed.

I had no appointments scheduled until 2pm, but with the rain outside, I was sure they would be dropping off my schedule. Sure enough, as I check my phone, my 2pm had canceled and my 3:30pm was asking for a literal "rain check."

I yawned and trekked across the bedroom in my underwear, casting my shadow in the blue white light lazing in from the windows. My eyes stung in the kitchen when I flicked on the incandescent bulbs. Thunder rolled outside as I scrambled myself some breakfast, and with it, my phone buzzed a few more times. Three clients had canceled. My full day just turned into an empty one.

Around eight, I gave Corey a call to see if he wanted to meet for coffee. He stayed in DC with a new 'friend' of his so he agreed to take the Metro to my area and meet me for coffee before he journeyed back to Sophia's where he was staying.

"So what'd you think about last night?" He asked as we sat down at a table in Pentagon City area. I stirred the cream into my coffee.

"I don't know what to say," I said. "A part of me wants to say that we experienced a squatter, but another part of me knows better. I don't know."

"It had to be Cook," Corey said. "This close to Samhain. It had to be."

"What does Samhain have to do with it?"

"The veil is the thinnest." Corey started and pantomimed a curtain rising from the table. "Spirits can cross into our world and we can cross into theirs."

"That's kind of creepy."

"It is what it is."

"I should let Peter and Nasaide know. I'm seeing them next full moon…"

"No," Corey said flatly.

"I don't understand. Is it some kind of secret?"

"They wouldn't understand. They're all about white light and love and things like that. To them, what we did may be seen as disrespectful to the dead."

I thought on this. Was the rest of the community so judgmental?

"My Feri teacher wouldn't mind so much."

"Maybe not. Feri is left-hand. They typically don't buy into white light dogma."

I shook my head, "What is with you and this anti-white light people?"

He chuckled, "Ah, I see."

"See what?"

"You haven't met them yet."

I shrugged, "Were there any at the Lughnasadh ritual or at any of the full moon meditations I went to with the Druid group?"

Corey sipped his coffee, "No one vocal. It's the really vocal ones that annoy the hell out of me. You'll see. You'll see."

It didn't feel right to tell Justin about the haunted house, in our October video chat session a few weeks later. This was something between Corey and me, and I felt Corey liked it that way. What I did tell Justin the next time we chatted was about how well I had adapted to the exercises he gave me and how simple but deep I found them to be. I hoped I wasn't coming off as a brown-noser, but I was sincere and very grateful.

"All of what you're saying sounds good," Justin said. He smiled on my laptop with tussles of blonde hair meshed down to his eyes. "I'm going to give you two more exercises I want you to do with the other exercises I've sent you. Take your time with them."

I was excited. Other than a ritualized prayer, I only had a grounding and a relaxation exercise. I supposed they were to prepare me for something bigger later.

Time went by quickly early October. The clients were good, my relationship with June was good, the exercises were good, however, the magic aspect was still questionable to me. I wanted to be sure that what I was experiencing was magic.

I was hoping to ask Nasaide and Peter what their opinion on it was and I kicked myself for not asking Justin when I had him on video chat. Unfortunately, their full moon get-together was canceled for this month due to Nasaide getting sick. I would have to wait until Samhain.

Lucky for me things were going as well as they were. I spent my free time with my nose in books. My collection already didn't fit into my trunk as well and I gave in and bought a large bookshelf to go in the guest room.

June's reactions to my bookcase were hard to read. She seemed pleased that I had something I was genuinely excited about, but reserved about the topic altogether. I respected this and did my best to keep my practice to myself. Witchcraft, as a rule, wasn't evangelical anyway.

Outside in the District, leaves began to change and descend. There was a color that the leaves reached here that I had never experienced in California. In Southern California, leaves would change to dull oranges and browns, but here, just as in springtime, the trees exploded with vibrant color. Some looked almost electric in the sunlight.

I took longer walks. Sometimes, passing right by my apartment in the evening and continuing down to the parks to breathe in the little nature I had around me. I imagined the entire city covered with vines and trees, overrun with green: the monuments, the capitol building, they would all look so much more beautiful if encroached upon by the goddess of the wild.

Everything meant something. A blue bird feather on the sidewalk was a gift from the Blue god. A cat that walked up to me and brushed against my leg was a greeting from Bast. Thunder in the sky was Thor. I didn't worship these beings, mind you. Worship is not part of the craft. I respected them as beings more powerful than I, yet because we are all eternal, they were beings that were no higher than I.

October reached its late days and suddenly I received invitations to various Halloween get-togethers.

"Sam and Ben have a Halloween party at their place this Friday," June said. She was in her nightgown, peeking into the living area. I had on a video game and I paused it and watched her. She rested her head on the door frame, exposing her slender neck. "Can you come?" she asked.

"I have a thing," I started. It was Lenore's group, the Green Man Tribe, Samhain gathering. It was supposed to be one of the bigger rituals of the year. "You should come with me. It'll be fun."

June yawned. "Another time. I really want to go to Sam and Ben's."

I hesitated, "did you want me to cancel?"

"No. You go do your thing." She said tersely and she turned to the hallway and began to walk away.

"Hey," I called to hear and I slipped over the hardwood floor in my socks and stumbled into the hallway. She was halfway to the bedroom when I wrapped my arms around her waist and whispered in her ear.

"I love you. If you ask me to cancel, I will do it."

I felt her tense up and then relax. She turned into me.

"No," she said, "I don't mind you going to this 'thing,' whatever it is, but just remember you have me to be with too. Don't forget about me."

"Never," I said and I kissed her and we swayed to the dark silence in the apartment until she took my hand and lead me into the bedroom.

9

There were drums. I heard them in the brisk Virginia air across the open fields. Lenore owned the property, a farmhouse with a huge tract of land hidden behind trees. The closest neighbor was several blocks away.

I parked my silver hatchback in the gravel lot bordered by a log fence and walked to the house, a one story with wooden sidings. There was a garden and a little sign out front said "Do not disturb the faeries."

Sophia let me in. She wore garb that looked like something from a Renaissance Faire.

"Jacob! How are you? It's so good to see you!" She embraced me and kissed me on the cheek. She smelled like wine and cookies.

Inside, the house was decorated with antiques and crystals. There were too many people standing about to get specific details: A splash of quartz here, an old miner's lantern there.

Lenore stood in the center of the very open living room. She raised a glass of wine at me while holding the hand of her partner, who I believed was named Anna. Anna's slender frame looked sickly next to Lenore, who had her thick, wild hair unrestrained and tasseled in all directions.

I recognized a few others from the Druid group and their full moon rituals. I mingled with them a bit before heading for the home-made mead. It was deliciously sweet and flavored with pumpkin.

"Jacob! How are you, handsome?" Lenore pulled me from the snack table and planted a kiss on my forehead. She introduced me to some of the members of her Green Man Tribe, mainly the drummers who I heard on arrival. One was named Jason, surprisingly ordinary considering the other two went by Talon and Phoenix.

"So who taught you to drum?" I thought it was an easy ice breaker question.

"No one did. I taught myself," Jason said. "The goddess taught me. I went to a party once and someone handed me a drum and I just went with it. My soul comes out when we get in a circle and drum. I love it. You should try it."

"Sure, if you don't mind."

"But after the ritual."

"Is the ritual typically energetic?"

"Not really. It's Samhain. We honor the dead—our loved ones. It's very solemn. That's why we have an after-party to liven the mood. Is this your first one?"

"Yes, I'm new to paganism so this is my first Samhain."

He smiled at me. "Welcome to the community."

Lenore called out for the ritual to start and we herded outside to a live fire pit. A table rested nearby with candles and pictures, hundreds of them, lain out into the flickering fire light. It was hard to see who was in the circle we formed. Faces darkened to deep red as someone turned out the porch lights.

Lenore told us all to ground and reach our center. I closed my eyes and imagined my thoughts drifting away from me. I imagined my body charging with red hot energy that kept me weighted and connected to the earth. I imagined the divine part of me, the part that floated like a halo above my head, charging with blue fire and surrounding me with love. I was grounded.

A woman circled us, a sword pointed outward to mark the boundaries of our ritual space. I watched her curiously. Many in the group had their eyes closed, some with their hands drawn out to their sides, giving energy to the circle.

Four designated people called to the guardians in each direction.

Then the Goddess and God were called with incantations from a male and female standing on either side of the fire pit, wearing dark cloaks. When they were done, the crowd stood in silence for a moment while Lenore walked to the center of the circle, next to the table with the pictures.

She began, "We gather this night, at the time of Samhain when the veil is at its thinnest, to honor those who have passed from this life to the next."

The ritual continued. Lenore described our role in the ritual, each taking an herb from a basket and tossing it into the fire while thinking of our loved ones. It was a somber event. I thought of my grandparents who passed away when I was still in high school. By the time the basket came to me, I was fighting tears.

The ritual ended with ceremonial 'cakes and ale' which was actually a plate of cookies and some wine. What was left over was placed on the altar of pictures as an offering.

"So must it be," Lenore said. The crowd repeated.

Afterward, the altar for the deceased was moved, respectfully, to a quiet corner with candles burning for those who wanted to leave offerings or add to it. The central fire was changed, however. Chairs circled around. People either sat on them or cuddled on blankets in the cool grass.

The drums began again as they had been playing when I had first arrived. Being so close to them now, I felt the rhythm in my bones. Jason was with them. One person would start off a beat and the others would follow suit in what was a harmonious mess of percussion. It was a living thing, the beat, sometimes rising in speed, sometimes slowing to a comfortable walk. A few in the grass started dancing to it. Some had other instruments—bells, woodblocks— and they pitched in when they could.

"Try it," Jason handed me his drum and patted his chair. We swapped places and he shouted into my ear, "just feel it. Let it take you."

I closed my eyes. At first there was nothing. I felt only anxiety at being put on the spot so readily. I held Jason's bulbous conga drum between my legs and could feel the beat of the other players, there were five of them, through the wooden body of the drum. I opened my eyes and caught sight of the others, Talon on a pair of bongos, Phoenix on another conga, watching me, nodding at me, smiling. The three others were lost in their rhythm.

Like a herd of stampeding horses, the drummers changed direction. They slowed to a trot. I joined them, timid quiet at first, barely striking the drums head with my palms but then the others got louder and I found myself beating my drum equally.

I watched the others. Their heads were lifted up and their eyes closed. It was like they were in a trance or maybe even having an orgasm. I closed my eyes too and soon the beat became a flash of colors behind my eyelids, blues and reds, yellows and greens. It was alive and I was moving with it, contributing to it. The speed and the rhythm changing and without much thought I followed it. The six of us were as one.

I heard some clapping and when I opened my eyes I saw a figure coming from the doorway followed by Lenore. It was Nasaide. She was dressed in a silk tunic exposing her protruding stomach. She continued toward us, stepping with our beat. When she reached the fire she stopped, raised her hands to her sides and began to dance with her pregnant belly.

It was like watching a goddess pregnant with the god of summer. She waved her arms and the beat slowed to allow her to move more seductively. She smiled at me and I smiled back.

We continued the beat on into the night until the fire died down and the crowd thinned to those remaining to sober up. Jason remained behind and he played a low beat being the last drummer.

"Are you a Druid or a shaman or something?" I asked as we sat near the fire.

"What do you mean?"

"In paganism. What are you?"

"I'm Jason," he winked. He took a long sip of his beer. "I am."

"Do you do some kind of magic?" I asked him.

He smiled at this. "Magic," he laughed.

"You don't believe in it?"

"Oh, I believe in it. Very much I believe in magic. It changed my life but you ask about magic as if it were something to do."

"I don't understand." I truly didn't.

"Magic," Jason started, "is something you become. It becomes you. Practicing magic is an expression of yourself and your own power. At least that's my opinion."

I heard Nasaide vocalize an agreement. She sat on a chair with Peter giving her a slow neck massage. She had a blanket over herself.

"Mmmm," she said. "Magic will change your life. It will lift you up and have you feeling like you're invincible, and it will throw you down to face your demons. Magic will ruin marriages, friendships, careers, and what you know of your life, but it always leads you to something better. How can it not? It's a part of you. It's what led me to my handsome husband." She looked up at Peter and they kissed.

I spent the remainder of the night in quiet contemplation.

10

Corey sat across from me at a diner in old town Alexandria. After Samhain, the weather took a change for the cold and Corey demonstrated this with his sweater and thick jacket which he still wore despite being indoors.

"Aren't you going to take that off?" I asked him.

"I'm okay."

The diner was a trendy one with a customer make-up of more yups and college students.

"I went to that Samhain with the Green Man Tribe." I said offhandedly.

Corey raised an eyebrow, "really, how was that?"

"It was great," I defied. "I met a guy that had a great deal to say about magic, how it's actually a state of being and we are magic. I liked it."

"I could have told you all that." He looked off to the side.

"It would have been cool if you showed up. What do you have against the group anyway?"

"I don't really like Lenore. She's meddlesome. Sophia was there and I've seen enough of her."

"Oh, right. Sophia. She seems like a very nice person." I said, dismissing whatever drama Corey had with her.

"Yeah."

After our meal we walked along Alexandria's crooked brick sidewalks. We reached the pier at the end that acts as a dock for some of the touristy boats and even a ferry to National Harbor. We walked along the roped barriers. I smelled the stale water and felt the cold wind against my face.

I thought to myself, If I am magic, what can I accomplish?

June wasn't feeling like going out so I took myself to a bookstore later that evening. One of the last remaining chains that hasn't been choked away by internet shopping. I found a small coffee shop inside and I ordered something light from the barista, a thick brunette with a sour face.

After grabbing a small cup of water from the condiment stand, I sat down in a corner with my back to no one. Music played over the speakers. One of them rattled at the bass. A child colored in a book with her mother nearby. Some middle-aged women huddled a few tables together and were chatting and laughing. More customers showed up and soon the place was busy with commotion.

I sipped quietly and surveyed the crowd some more. A man in a green tee shirt talked loudly to someone on speaker phone. A mother walked in with two children who ran across the shop, one of them bumped my table. And that's what set me off.

"Sorry," the mother said to me offhanded. She yelled at her kids to stop running. They didn't listen.

I watched my coffee, still rippling with the table bump.

Relax. Relax.

I thought of the ocean. I pictured empty forests with trickling streams.

Not here. Not now.

The cafe area seemed to get louder. The music too. I heard the kids screaming and laughing, the women cackling, even the coloring child near me was scraping crayons loudly. The walls closed in. The ceiling dropped. I felt hot. I felt cold. Beads of sweat dribbled down my forehead.

Relax. Relax.

"No!" the man on the speakerphone shouted. One of the children knocked his coffee over. There was a commotion. The mother apologized profusely.

"I told you two to stop running in here!" she shouted at her brats.

Just breathe. Just breathe.

A group of younger adults walked in, talking loudly. Moving slowly. Blocking the way out of the shop.

Relax. Breath.

A panic attack in a bookstore was not what I needed. Not after feeling so good these past few days. Not after the tremendous high that paganism brought me, that the Craft brought me. The wave of tension was building up and soon it would hit me and then I'd… what? pass out? Put my head down? Scream? *Scream.*

I reached for my water cup. I thought of an exercise Justin had given me. One that involved just water and some breathing. It's called Kala.

I allowed these anxious thoughts to build in me. The children screaming and running around. "*Ohb,*" they would say. "Water." They used to run to the street looking for handouts as we drove across the dirt roads of their desert. "*Ohb!*"

Explosions. I could hear them in the coffee shop as they happened in my head, in Afghanistan. My teeth chattered. My spine chilled with death. "*Ohb,*" the children would say.

When I felt these feelings were reaching a climax, I blew them into the water in front of me. I could feel their weight emptying from my belly. The clear water rippled. The coloring child nearby looked up for a moment to watch me.

I'm just a guy blowing into a cup of water. Nothing to see here. Keep coloring.

You would think that I was done. The negative energy was exhaled. Why bother with anything else? But Feri witchcraft teaches you to face your fears, not run from them, not expel them.

I concentrated on the color blue, imagining it lick around me in flames. It's called blue fire because it's the the spark of life. It's the spark that started all of creation. The color that carries all other colors just as the blue sky can carry all colors from sunset and sunrise, light and dark. Just like the sky can carry a rainbow.

I let these flames build up, closing my eyes to allow the visual. *Just a guy closing his eyes in front of a cup of water. Don't mind me.*

Blue fire licked up my body and into my pores. I felt it building up in my belly and in my sex. It was warm, powerful, tingling. I continued to breathe it in. It empowered me and strengthened me. It rose up to my hands and I could feel my palms heat up. *Is this real?*

It rotated around my wrists and between my fingers. When I felt the blue fire had reached a significant charge, I placed both hands over my water cup and imagined my blue fire purging the water of my anxiety.

The water began to glow a brilliant white in my mind's eye. The foul blackness of my panic attack had melted away. I drank the water, now cleansed of my worries. I drank it because in Kala we know that our problems are ours. It is our energy. We don't give our energy away, we cleanse it. I pictured this now stable energy running through my limbs and circling my belly—icy hot fire trailing across my body.

If I am magic, I can do anything I set my will to.

I willed the anxiety out of me. I watched it fade away into calm, white energy that illuminated my soul. It no longer controlled me. I sat in silence, allowing the experience of Kala to continue until I felt ready to open my eyes.

Nothing changed in the coffee shop. The crowd was still as rambunctious as before. The children were still screaming while the mother picked up her coffee and tried in vain to usher them back out to the bookstore. The young adults joked and laughed, some wrestled lightly with jabs to the shoulder.

I smiled as I finished my coffee.

When I got home June was reading a book on the sofa. She looked up at me as I walked in the door, a grimace on her face.

"What's wrong?" I asked.

"I have some news you might not like," she said.

THE WHEEL AND THE DAY

I tossed my keys into the bowl near the door and took off my jacket. June waited for me patiently which meant the news was worse than I expected.

When I sat down next to her, after planting a kiss on her forehead, she said, "my mother is coming up for Thanksgiving."

"Oh," I started. I wondered if I could Kala this situation away. "...shit."

11

I thought about the dreaded Carmen well until the next full moon. What do I do? How do I handle this woman?

Druid full moon ritual fell on a Saturday and I was glad for it. Some pagans practice their full moons with a coven, if they're lucky enough to find a coven to be in. I had no such luck and the Druid full moon rites were, for the most part, informal affairs that didn't require much in terms of commitment or secrecy.

Nasaide and Peter played the roles of High Druids. Nasaide with a bit of grace and Peter with his charm. I admired them.

Corey was there. He showed up with Sophia and I somehow guessed he showed up knowing I would be there too.

Afterward we spread out in the dining room for our full moon potluck. Sophia, with good intentions, chatted with Nasaide, and Peter had some new members he tried to make feel comfortable. I crept next to Corey at the table.

"I need to ask you something?"

"Oh, yeah? What?"

"I need to know what to do about my girlfriend's mother. She's coming over for Thanksgiving and she hates my guts."

Corey laughed. "You want her not to come?"

I thought about it. "No, that would upset June. I just want her to be nicer or to just stop insulting me every chance she gets."

"You can try a honey jar spell," Nasaide said. She looked pleased to get away from Sophia. Nasaide scooted near us and sat down in a chair. Her belly shadowing over her thin legs. She patted herself. "A honey jar spell works if you want to make someone sweet on you."

"But you need something of the person or a picture to place at the bottom of the jar," Corey interjected. "Can you find anything like that?"

I shook my head, "June would notice if I took a picture from her photo album."

"What about an online profile?" Nasaide chimed in.

"Carmen is social media terrified. She thinks the government is after her information."

"Well," Corey said, "in a pinch you could always place an onyx stone under her. It'll bind her from doing you harm."

"Really?" I said. "That works. I have a few onyx stones at home too."

Corey explained how the process worked. I had to activate the stone by appealing to its spirit.

"The stone has a spirit?"

"Everything has a spiritual substance to it," Nasaide broke in. "It's part of working with the honey in the honey jar spell too. You need to speak with or empathize with the spirit of whatever substance you're working with. It's how you get the substance to do the working for you."

"Interesting." I said.

Later that evening I found myself sitting with only the two newcomers in the group. They introduced themselves as Veronica and Andrew. They didn't come together but I could tell they hit it off in all the right ways.

They both spoke about the 'energy' of the group and how inviting that energy was.

"I can read auras" Veronica said. "You have a very unique one. Do you know what your special gift is?"

"My special gift?"

"Yes, we all have at least one, something you're good at and meant to do."

"Can't say I know what that is just yet."

I looked to Andrew who was smiling broadly as if to say "Isn't she great?"

Veronica started talking more about the energy of each individual person and how it made the whole of the group. I was half paying attention when I started picking up on a peculiar vibe, myself.

There was tension, somewhere in the house and I could feel it. But I didn't know how I was sensing it. There was just an eerie chill at the base of my spine and a sour sensation in the pit of my stomach but it was also more than that. I could feel unease in the space around me coming from somewhere else.

Veronica kept prattling on and I excused myself for the restroom. The feeling of tension was stronger in the hallway. I crept along the wooden floors until I reached the restroom opposite what we called "the ritual room." The ritual room door was open and I heard voices sounding like low growls. Two male and two female. I knew it was Peter and Corey at the center of it.

Corey said something along the lines of "this is unfair judgment."

I heard Peter say, "You don't respect the community and you have little regard for those who have helped you thus far. We want to help you but you have some lessons to learn from where you're at."

"And you're the one's to decide that for me?" Corey raised his voice just a little.

I heard the soft coo of Sophia's voice mutter something and Corey let out a scoff.

It was Nasaide's turn to chime in, "This is the attitude we're talking about."

As quietly as I could, I let myself into the restroom, feeling embarrassed at myself for having listened this long to their conversation. I closed the door, but not before catching eyes with Corey from the other side of the hallway.

When Carmen arrived, she hardly looked at me. We picked her up at Reagan National and had to run inside to find her because she refused to stand out on the sidewalk.

"Carmen, it's good to see you," I said when I saw her, knowing damn well she would ignore me.

She looked quickly to June, "*Mija!*" She started and kissed June on the cheek. As she and June headed to the car, Carmen left her luggage for me to carry. I really hoped the onyx spell would work.

At home, Carmen went on her usual complaining about the plane ride and how congested she felt with the dry air blowing from the small personal vents and how she would get hot if it wasn't on. She never looked at me or acknowledged me, which I was sure was a good thing.

She let me put her luggage in the guest room. I hid all of my ritual magic stuff in my own bedroom this time so she wouldn't go through any of it. I pulled out an onyx stone and left it on my dresser for later. Carmen was just warming up. She'd have more to say as the day wore on.

It wasn't until later that evening that she started to dig in. She sat on my beige chair with her hands folded over her belly. Her bare veiny feet rolled over my carpet. June had on a cooking show with some thin model chef showing how easy it is to bake a turkey. June described how she wanted to fry the turkey this year and went into detail of how she wanted to make the stuffing.

Carmen licked her fuzzy upper lip and turned to me, "What are you going to do tomorrow? Just sit on the couch and watch the game?"

It wasn't enough to cause June to look up from her program but I knew that Carmen started off with a light chisel, pecking away at the sore spots she thought you had. This one was meant to be emasculating.

"I'll be making the string bean casserole," I said quietly. "You know I don't really care much for sports."

"Men normally watch the game." She said bluntly and there

was a hint of a smile on her face. So pleased with herself. Still too subtle to catch June's attention.

I could point it out. I could bring June in to referee, but then what kind of a child would that make me? Besides, June seemed oblivious to Carmen's hatred of me—her hatred of all men as far as I could tell.

I brought it all up once after one of Carmen's extended stays.

"You know what I think? I think you have a problem with strong women," June said smartly.

I hated when women used this excuse. As if females were incapable of being assholes or as if people that behaved this way were behaving like real men. No one I knew did. But I am, in the eyes of alpha males and allegedly "strong" women, a beta man. I don't like sports. I don't demand the approval or the respect from others. I don't care enough to. I don't have a managerial position at some big wig company wearing five-hundred dollar suits and clacking shoes. I don't speak with authority or condescension.

"I don't have a problem with you as a strong woman," I retorted. June just stuck her tongue out.

Just you wait until tomorrow, I thought to myself, watching Carmen shuffle her heavy frame in my chair, as she watched the food channel with practically fogged up glasses. I headed to the bedroom, hearing Carmen mutter something under her breath that sounded like, "run away, little boy."

It rained the next day, Thanksgiving Day. I woke up with June taking up most of the bed as usual. I kissed her forehead and stretched rolling naked out from under the soft feather comforter. There was a chill in the air and I tossed on a robe and stepped lightly over the soft carpet to the black stone on the dresser.

"Today is the day," I said to myself.

I spent the morning avoiding Carmen altogether. I wanted to be in a good mood during Thanksgiving dinner. She eyed me a few times, said a few things under her breath, but I heard none of it.

June insisted on making the turkey. She was looking forward to trying out something new that she said would dazzle our taste buds. Carmen worked on some cranberry sauce that was some sort of staple with her family. I put together the green bean casserole which was always my favorite part of Thanksgiving dinner.

With the sides done and only the turkey and a pumpkin pie in the oven, I slipped away to the bedroom and picked up the onyx stone. Holding it in my hand, I envisioned a pulsing aura emanating from its center and gliding over its uneven face.

I started speaking to the stone, feeling a little silly at first, but gaining confidence as I remembered the point of this exercise: "Onyx, stone of black, guard the lips of Carmen during this meal, bind her tongue, bind her speech." Imagining its aura awakened by my words, I rubbed my fingers over the surface of the stone, using the oils of my fingers to polish it.

Back in the kitchen, Carmen was setting the table while June was pulling out the Turkey. The room was tangled with the aromas of roasted turkey, pumpkin spice, and cranberry sauce. I casually walked up to the table and helped Carmen place silverware. She stopped for a moment and watched me disdainfully. She shrugged it off and continued setting down a tiles for the hot food. When she turned to grab some napkins, I dropped the onyx near her usual seat and rolled it neatly beneath the chair.

"Honey, can you put the food on the table?" June asked me. I did just that, making sure to place the turkey dead center. Carmen muttered quietly to herself near the stuffing adding some salt and other spices.

Have a seat Carmen, I thought to myself.

To my horror, she did just that, in June's seat.

"What are you doing?" I asked, suddenly.

"I'm so tired. I was on my feet all day," she said and she kicked off her shoes under the table.

"But," I started, but it was useless. June turned around with the cranberry sauce and sat down in her mother's usual seat.

I carved the turkey in silence, not sure how my spell would play

83

out. June didn't say a word while in her new seat, but neither did her mother.

The wording of the spell was intended for Carmen, so it shouldn't have an effect on June, should it? But June was so quiet. Was she always this quiet? Not a word. She also looked uncomfortable, didn't she?

I decided to start some conversation. Maybe it was just my imagination, "Are you hungry, babe?"

"Mm hmm." She nodded, a peculiarly laconic answer given the circumstance.

I served Carmen first. "Is that enough, Carmen. Would you like more?" I asked her giving her an opportunity to put me down, say something, anything.

"Yes, that is enough," she said. She, too, seemed uncomfortable, her face in a small grimace and her eyes looking nowhere near me.

We each reached for the food in silence, passing it around as if in a spiritist's dumb supper. All that could be heard were the scraping of metal forks and ceramic plates.

"I had a good week this week with work," I made another pass at small talk. "I'm surprised so close to a holiday. Normally people are less interested in paying for a massage during this period."

June chewed her food, but nodded. It was Carmen who responded, "Good job." There was an awkward silence after she said it and I could see on her face the same uncomfortable grimace that was there earlier. She stammered, but in her Spanish accent she said, "maybe some people need a good massage therapist when there is no home to go to."

I was shocked. Not only was she acknowledging me, she offered a compliment. Maybe the spell was working, but in a different way than I anticipated. Maybe the blood link between Carmen and June was making the spell effective. Or maybe I was reading too much into this. But June still had not said a word and Carmen seemed ...kind.

I saw Carmen pick through my green bean casserole and I

asked her, "how are the green beans? I hope they're not soggy."

"Delicious," she said and then she struggled again, looking surprised at her own words, "you both are terrific cooks. Very good food."

The spell worked. I had to admit it. Carmen was never this way. June smiled, she even placed a hand on her mother's arm, but she said nothing.

I'm sorry, June, I said to myself. We ate the remainder of our food in happy silence.

Later, that night, June asked me how I thought dinner went. I had already discreetly swiped the onyx stone from underneath June's seat before anyone noticed it.

"It was great, if just a little quiet," I responded, feeling some guilt for June.

"God, yes," June started, "I'm sorry about that. I was just so nervous. I had a talk with my mother about being nicer to you. I didn't expect her to actually listen."

12

I spent the next few days giving June and Carmen some space.
Carmen wanted to visit some of the monuments as always and I
opted out. She remained awkwardly silent when I was around and
it actually made me feel uneasy. I thought maybe I went too far
with the spell and that it was somehow affecting her actual free
will. Sure I was kind to Carmen. I said my "good mornings" and
"thank yous," For a while I convinced myself that my spell didn't
work and that Carmen's silence had more to do with June's plea
with her to be nicer. Maybe it was a passive aggressive attempt at
stating that there was nothing kind to say to me. There was still
something unnatural about it. Good or evil, I was still happy with
the results. Thanksgiving weekend was proving to be one of the
most relaxing times for me. Carmen left Monday morning. She
hugged me and thanked me for the wonderful Thanksgiving. Even
June was shocked by it.

Giving June and Carmen more space as they headed to the
airport, I went for a jog around the neighborhood. The air around
Pentagon Row was crisp and chilled my throat as I paced my way
around the crowded areas and closer to the quieter residential
apartments off Fern Street. The few remaining brilliant October
leaves had died out to rustic brown. Most littered the sidewalk and
curbsides as I crunched to a small pocket of shops off 23rd Street
and then back into a few blocks of quietly colored colonial style
houses.

I love October most, but November has its charm too. There's
always this sense of goodbye in November here in the DC area.

Mother Nature and Father Time reminisce about their lives in November. They embrace as the last leaves drop dead, and then they fall fast asleep to the standstill times of Winter, to be woken up in time for Spring.

I imagined what pagans in the past had done to honor this. I suppose it was closer to what Samhain actually meant: the slaughter of livestock to save as food for the winter and maybe a bonfire or two both to cook with and to dance around. It seemed so practical I hardly considered it spiritual.

As I ran back up Joyce Street, back toward my apartment, I realized that the more information I knew about magic and witchcraft, the less "magical" it seemed to become. Where was the real mystery, and not the New Age banter I kept hearing about? I thought about my spell on Carmen and how it seemed to coincide with June asking her to behave. Did I cause that? Was that part of my spell? Corey did mention that magic chooses the path of least resistance. Maybe my spell planted a seed of thought in June's mind, prompting her to speak with her mother.

I shook my head. It all sounded like too much... power. If my thoughts were correct, then I can easily manipulate someone else with a spell, which means anyone else is capable of manipulating me or a loved one with a spell. But it was harmless, wasn't it? It was just a spell of peace and quiet, right?

I passed the park off Joyce street and slowed to a walk. There were no small children out, but I did see a bunch of teenagers playing basketball and group of young adults playing soccer. What if someone cast a spell to cause harm to these people? Would something intervene? Would someone?

Magic is dangerous, I thought. If it worked the way I thought it did, no wonder people feared magical working in the past.

After my shower at home, I checked my phone and realized I had a text message from an unrecognized number. It read, "I was just invited to a social with Inner Fire tomorrow late afternoon. Want to come?"

"Who is this?" I typed back.

"It's Jason Cedar, from Samhain."

I met Jason at the Gallery Place metro stop in DC. He showed up in a bright red hoodie. Strands of dirty blond hair poked out from beneath his string tightened hood. He had grown a wild looking beard since I last saw him. It made him look artsy. We walked passed the Friendship Arch, the gate that leads into Chinatown. I loved the smells there. The various restaurants had vents leading from their kitchens to the sidewalk where we could smell all of the chicken dumplings and fried rice and sweet pork carrying throughout the area.

Jason was obviously freezing cold. We experienced a cold snap the night before and temperatures plummeted from a cool 50 degrees to freezing 25.

"You want to stop in one of these places and get some coffee or something?" I asked him.

"No, we're not far."

"Okay."

He led me to a massive American sandwich shop that seemed quite empty except for a group sitting at the shop's corner tables. We were greeted by a young woman with deep red hair and freckles, wearing a black tee shirt with "Liberal Feminist and Proud" written on it in rainbow colors. She introduced herself as "Chamomile" or "Cham," for short.

"Welcome to our interest meeting," she smiled. I saw a piece of her smile fade away as she looked me over. She seemed to really like Jason. Jason pulled back his hood revealing a yarn stitched beanie on his head. Maybe she thought he looked the hipster part?

There were others sitting at the bench-like tables. Most were caught up in their own conversations. A few smiled our direction. I didn't get a negative vibe from anyone. I did feel out of place with my slogan-free shirt and military style haircut I revealed after pulling off my plain black beanie.

"I'm Raven" a heavy set girl with bouncing short black hair greeted me. I smiled and shook her hand as she explained, "I'm part of the central group of Inner Fire."

"Ah, another Raven," I said heartily. "It's a pleasure meeting you."

I could tell by her immediate frown that I had just offended her. Maybe commenting on how common someone's attempt to be unique is, wasn't the politest thing to do. She shook Jason's hand then heaved herself back toward the group at the tables.

"What did you do, step on her little dog?" Jason whispered at me.

"I accidentally forgot how sensitive folks were about their magical names."

"Ah..." Jason winced. "It's best not to comment on their names at all. Don't even show that it phases you. It took me a while to get used to that."

"Do you have a magical name?" I asked Jason.

"My last name is Cedar. Do I really need one?"

I chuckled, getting an awkward glance from Raven.

There were about a dozen other people there, but I couldn't remember all of their names and being as uncomfortable and feeling as out of place as I was, I didn't really put in a whole lot of effort. A dark-skinned girl in an orange pattern shirt and purple skirt approached me. She called herself "Pearl."

"I'm a librarian here in DC," she explained.

I eyed her earrings which looked like they were made of fishing wire and a rainbow of stones.

"Do you like them?" she asked. "I made them myself."

"What do they mean?" I started. "I mean, do they mean anything particular."

"There's one for each chakra. They're for balancing my power centers."

"I see. Do you feel that it works?"

"It helps. It definitely helps."

A young man with dark features and a rolling gut, calling himself "Cu," short for "Cu Chulain," was next. He described himself as a class of warrior witch that fought the forces of evil, and I have to admit that the idea sounded pretty interesting to me.

"Are there a lot of bad guys keeping you busy?" I asked, a bit unsure of how "bad guys" came off.

Cu's face lit up. "Oh there is a lot of negative energy here in the District. Just look at our legislative branch. I have to work extra hard to keep them in line, but it's tiring work. I'm all alone."

Those words floated a while just outside his mouth: "I'm all alone." I'm sure there were hundreds of witches, Wiccans, and other spell casting pagans who sent magic very regularly down to the Capitol.

"I'm sure you're not alone, Cu. I'm sure lots of folks cast."

"Not all of them do it enough," he went on to talk about how he felt he was called to fight the evils in Congress by his deceased father, who was a screaming liberal who passed away without healthcare. I empathized with him, but I felt he was a bit off. It seemed the others did as well. Cu and I were catching some giggles and eye rolls as we talked.

I thanked him for feeling comfortable talking to me about his struggles with the evils of Congress.

"Let me know if you ever want to join me," he called out as I went to find Jason.

The sandwich shop was full of diverse witches and I felt a tinge of pride at seeing the numbers and the variety. Cham was doing an excellent job making sure everyone felt welcome. Her immediate reaction to me must have changed because I caught a few smiles from her. I overheard one of the male witches call her Esther and I wondered how many Judeo-Christian names were hidden behind magical ones.

I finally found Jason in line at the sandwich counter, ordering a turkey on wheat. He was talking to a guy about my age, dressed in a black hoodie with dark brown hair, similar to mine. Jason introduced him as Gideon.

"It's my actual name," he said. "You'd be surprised how many folks ask me why I'd choose a magical name straight from the book of Judges."

I laughed at this.

Gideon was dating a girl he had met online in a massive multiplayer online role playing game. They first met at a halfway point in Richmond and the rest was gamer paradise.

"Samantha's playing right now as we speak. I'd be online doing a raid as well, but you know, have to see the sun at some point."

We sat at one of the few circular tables with attached chairs, only slightly away from the rest of the crowd. Jason chucked half of his foot long sandwich to me while Gideon sipped on some iced tea. We talked a bit about our spiritual paths. Gideon considered himself a traditional witch, but I was unsure what that meant. I told him how I was training in the Feri tradition, and he seemed to know exactly what that was.

"The Anderson's tradition. That's great," he said.

"Yeah, ole Victor and Cora. I'm training distance," I explained and I saw him wince.

"Don't go telling everyone about that. Some folks are very opinionated about how training should be done and blah blah blah." He circled a finger around a temple. "I don't care, obviously. Jason's done some of his training as distance training."

Jason nodded. I was curious to hear about his story

"I'm more interested in Druidry, some shamanism, and of course the craft," he said.

Gideon squeezed one of Jason's cheeks. "He's a little green witch, yes he is."

Jason swatted at him and there was a brief moment I thought the table would get knocked over by the two punching each other's arms. We got a few disapproving looks from the others but no one said anything.

"Oh hey," Gideon started, sounding a bit out of breath, "you guys want to go to a house warming party? It's for a few friends in Logan's Circle. I raised my eyebrows but I looked to Jason for a cue.

"Which friends are these?" Jason asked.

"Lois and William."

"Those are your new roommates!"

"Yeah, it's my house warming party."

Jason howled, "You dumbass. You are inviting us to your own housewarming party."

"Okay, shut up! Are you coming?"

"When is it," I asked.

"In about a half hour," Gideon said.

We thanked Chamomile for the event and headed out the door. I gave a quick wave to Cu who sat alone in a corner, staring at the floor. He was smiling about something.

On our way to Logan's Circle, Jason picked up a box of wine from a liquor store and handed it to Gideon.

"What the hell is this?" Gideon asked.

"It's your housewarming gift," Jason grinned.

"You cheap ass!"

"What?"

"Boxed wine? Who buys anyone boxed wine?"

"They had bagged wine, but I figured you were a slight step up from that."

"I'm not carrying a box of cheap wine into my own housewarming party. Here!"

Gideon tried passing the box back to Jason, but Jason stuffed his hands into his pockets. Gideon looked at me.

"Jake, you wouldn't let a man carry boxed wine to his own housewarming party, would you?"

"Jacob, put your hands in your pocket! Don't be a weenie!" Jason howled from the crosswalk.

I stuffed my hands into my hoodie front pockets. "Sorry man. I can't carry boxed wine. It'd make a horrible impression on people

I don't know."

"Assholes!"

Jason couldn't stop laughing, especially when we walked on to the Metro and folks started staring. A group of girls even pointed and laughed.

"This is like high school all over again," Gideon hung his head down and even I couldn't help but laugh.

Feeling bad for him, I ended up carrying the boxed wine through the door. Thankfully, no one noticed me much when I walked in. They were busy cheering on Gideon. Unable to find a clear path to the kitchen, I just hid the box under a night stand near the couch.

Gideon had definitely found a nice place with his roommates, Lois and William. The connected townhome was of the classic DC architecture. The inside was trimmed with decorative molding and a fireplace, which was guarded quietly by an iron fence. There was an old smell to the place and it reminded me of the Cooke house Cory and I went to. I felt a shiver run down my spine when I thought of it.

Video games were being played over one of the three consoles wired in to flat screen television. There was plenty of IPA beer floating around and it wasn't long before I was a little tipsy.

Gideon told us many of the party goers were pagan, despite his roommates atheistic, yet open-minded, tendencies. I recognized some of the guests from Lenore's Samhain rite.

"Pagans and atheists get along great!" Gideon said while motioning to Lois. William was out grabbing some wine.

"Hey, what did you do with the juice box?" Jason asked Gideon. Both of them were drunk at this point.

"What juice box? Didn't I hand that back to you?"

"You lost my juice box!" Jason punched Gideon on the arm and Gideon swatted back, catching only air.

"God! You two! Don't rough house! You're going to spill something," Lois started. "Seriously, how old are you both?"

"We're immature," Jason said quietly.

I felt a tug on my arm and I turned to see Corey standing by my side, smiling.

"Hey what are you doing here?" I asked him. I gave him a hug. As I did so I could see Lois approaching us and it was clear that Corey was connected to her. They hugged and chatted a bit while Jason and Gideon joked on the couch.

"Hey, Jacob. You know where my juice box is?" Jason asked.

I didn't answer. I figured he was drunk enough. No need to give him a hangover on cheap wine.

"So, what are you doing here? How do you know these guys?" Corey asked after Lois left the room.

"I know Jason from the Samhain ritual I told you about and Gideon, I just met early at the Inner Fire meetup."

"Inner fire, huh?" I could sense contempt in Cory's tone.

"They were really nice folks."

"Yeah, they're alright. They're a very eclectic group, if you're into that sort of thing."

Jason piped in from the couch, "There's nothing wrong with that."

"I didn't say there was," Cory retorted, a bit annoyed.

There was an awkward moment where Jason furrowed his brows and he and Gideon exchanged glances. Jason shrugged his shoulders and continued moaning about his juice box.

"So, when'd you get here?" I asked Corey, just for the sake of changing the atmosphere.

"A little while ago. I saw you but there was some rough housing near you so I waited till it was done. I didn't want to lose an eye." He was side-eyeing Jason and Gideon who looked at each other once again.

"What's with you?" I whispered under my breath to Corey.

"Rough-housing?" Gideon said suddenly. "Who's rough housing at this fine establishment?"

"Rough-housing?" Jason added. "Let me get my bat. I'll show 'em." For a second it looked like he was about to tackle Gideon, he had this devilish fire in his eyes. Then, he took a quick glance at Corey and then turned on me. I was on the ground suddenly with Jason on top of me, pinning me down with his legs. He rummaged through my hoodie pockets.

"My juice box! Where is it, Jakey Jake Jake!" He shouted.

I started laughing and Gideon suddenly tackled Jason, bumping Corey who stood up in disgust.

"I'll save you, Jake!" Gideon cried and we all started laughing.

I didn't see where Corey went after that and I didn't see him for the remainder of the party.

"Good riddance," I heard Gideon say. Both he and Jason were panting.

"What the hell is this?" I heard Lois from somewhere near the door entrance. I thought she was referring to our rough-housing and I got up pretty quick, feeling like a lousy house guest.

"We're immature," Jason laughed.

Lois held up Gideon's boxed wine, "which one of you brought this monstrosity?"

Jason howled, "My juice box!"

13

I mentioned Gideon's remark about distance learning to Justin on our next online video chat the following week. He seemed less than pleased I brought it up.

"There are plenty of people who have a very dogmatic view of how this stuff is supposed to be taught. But if you ask me, waiting around until you happen to run across another Feri initiate in person… well, the line would die off and we have to be practical. There is new technology we can use to help us keep our line strong. Why not use it?" He explained.

"That makes perfect sense," I assured him.

"Let's not worry about what others view us as anyway," he said while fixing his glasses. It was pretty cold in the DC Metro area, but I could tell Justin was nice and warm in California, wearing a light blue T-shirt. "The craft isn't about catering to someone else's dogmas," he paused. "Let's begin, shall we?"

I straightened in my chair and adjusted my web camera. I had a black candle ready to start our prayer and it began with some relaxation and grounding exercises followed by what was called a soul alignment, taking the aspects of myself and aligning them so I was more fully present. We recited the Star Goddess prayer and Justin lead me through a guided meditation where I followed a bird into a tree and walked along an earthen staircase inside of it. I journeyed down to the bowels of the earth where I met a young man painted in blue who approached me, nude and unashamed.

I thought of Adam and Eve. I thought of innocence before the fall of mankind and what that must have felt like, nudists without a care in the world. What did they do then when they ran out of things to do?

"Focus." Justin's voice entered my dream world like the voice of a god in the Garden of Eden.

(*Who told you you were naked!*)

"Your energy is all over the place," Justin whispered. "Stay focused."

I saw the man, painted in blue and naked. He bid me to follow him, running fast over wild blades of grasses and weeds and through thornless briars. We ran across deserts and forests and along endless splashing streams. We ran on all fours, like animals, and galloped painlessly over dusty rock and seeping clay. I was like a horse, untamed and wild in open fields. I kicked in ecstasy. Then we stopped. I was human again, naked, like the Blue God. We sat around a small fire and watched the sun go down.

"This is how it can be always," he said to me. "Let go."

"Of what?"

"Everything."

He melted into the darkening sky. His body spread across the horizon, but his eyes joined as one and twinkled as the evening star.

I told Justin about this experience after he guided me out of me trance.

"Yes, that sounds like him. The Blue God is very big on liberation and freedom."

"He said, 'everything,'" I explained. "That couldn't possibly be everything, right? Obviously I need to pay my bills and stuff like that if I expect to live in this society."

"True, but what the Blue God was probably considering is your attachments to those things and how much those things play a factor in what you can and can't do. 'Let go' could also be considered 'take control.'"

"That sounds contradictory."

"It is. But that doesn't make it 'untrue,' or 'inapplicable' if you prefer. Remember, the world isn't just a simple two dimensional line with points. It's winding and moving shapes. Put your fingers on opposite sides of a globe and turn the globe so that one point is directly in front of you while the other point is hidden behind it. To a linear thinker, they could be two different points overlapping and therefore must be the same, but yet they are contradictory. To someone who possess a heart of innocence, who sees the world for what it truly is, that person would understand that there are two separate points on a rotating orb and have aligned for a moment before returning to their regular course," he was looking up at the ceiling in his own room. He shook his head and smiled. "Do you understand?"

I nodded, "I think so. In a way they're both true. You need to have the perspective of the linear thinker as well as of the 'heart of innocence,' as you called it, in order to appreciate the contradiction and yet understand that it is just a matter of perspective."

"Very good."

We decided to end there.

"Jacob?" Justin said in closing.

"Yes?"

"Be careful that you don't wear yourself thin. I know paganism can be very exciting at first, but it's possible to try to commit to too many things at once and get nowhere with any of them. Just be mindful of that. Even if you decide Feri isn't your thing, just make sure you're progressing."

"Do you feel like I'm not progressing?"

"Of course not. You've come a long way in a short amount of time. You have a fire in you. The witch blood is coursing through you. It's just a general warning I'd give to anyone just starting out on their witch path."

"Wait, the witch blood?"

"We'll have to get into that another day. For now, keep with your daily practices and check in with me once a week."

"Will do."

THE WHEEL AND THE DAY

Yule, the Winter Solstice, was coming up and I wanted to see what was going on around the area. Jason would know of the more obscure gatherings of the sort that I was starting to crave, but I hadn't heard from Jason in a couple weeks and he didn't return my phone calls. I dismissed it as him being very busy with something.

The only group that had any announcements on social media was the Druid group. Nasaide was expecting her baby any day now and since Lenore, and even Sophia were set to attend, I figured I would check it out.

"Babe," I called out to the kitchen where June was fixing herself a bowl of cereal.

"Yeah?"

"You want to meet the pagan group I've been hanging out with? They're really nice. I'm sure they'd love to meet you."

There was silence. I thought I could hear the faint sounds of crunching.

"It's for their Yule. It's like Christmas," I added.

"Eh, that's okay. I'm really not big on that kind of stuff."

"Are you sure? It's just folks getting together, sacrificing a few virgins—which are hard to find in this day and age."

Her lack of laughter concerned me.

"Yeah, I'm sure. No thanks."

"Okay, babe. Just thought I'd ask, just in case."

At Peter and Nasaide's home, the walls were decorated in yew and Douglas fir branches tied with ribbons and small wicker balls with tiny scrolls tucked inside. Various herbs and mistletoe was everywhere and I suffered a few cheek kisses from men and women because of it. It really looked every bit like Christmas inside, except for the lack of nativity scenes or a Santa Claus.

"The Christians placed their Christmas holiday over Yule as an attempt to Christianize the pagan solstice holiday," Sophia explained. "Many of the old symbols of trees and elves and magic survived, though." She was rubbing her temples.

"Are you feeling okay?"

"I've been getting a lot of headaches lately," she said. "I'll be fine. Don't worry about me."

Lenore was happy to see me. I think she was just a little drunk too, but she was a comfortable drunk rather than a belligerent one.

"You couldn't manage to get June out here, this time?" Lenore seemed concerned.

"I tried, but she wasn't feeling up to it."

"Oh, give her some time," she said, her eyes showing a level of solemnity that was starting to concern me. "She just has to make it to one so she can see we don't, you know, sacrifice virgins, or any kind of nonsense like that."

I half laughed and fully blushed. Maybe I should avoid making jokes of that nature with June.

Nasaide sat in the dining room surrounded by well-wishers and "blessed be's." She kept touching her belly and rubbing it. I could hear her humming softly as folks talked to her. Peter stood close by. He looked worried about the overzealous people, but bit his lip as they slowly dispersed.

"Jacob," Nasaide called to me. "Jacob come here. It's so good to see you!"

She asked me about the binding spell and I told her about how June sat in her mother's seat instead and how concerned I was that June was so quiet, but so was her mother. I explained that June had a talk with her mother about being obnoxious and that was the real reason for the silence.

Nasaide laughed. It was hearty and I could see Peter loosening up and smiling. "I'm so sorry," she heaved, wiping a tear from her left eye. "It's just so perfect."

"Do you think the spell worked?"

"Oh, yes, of course it did. Magic uses the path of least resistance. That meant using your girlfriend to get her mother to pipe down."

"You don't suppose I messed with their free will, though, do you? I mean, was that bad magic?"

"I would hardly say so. It *was* a binding spell, but it was well intentioned. A peaceful Thanksgiving is well-intentioned in my opinion anyway. You really didn't harm anyone. As for 'bad' magic, please. We play in the gray." She chuckled a bit.

I smiled at her.

"So, how are you doing?" I asked.

She had her eyes closed and she was rubbing her stomach again.

"I think he's about ready. Any day. Maybe as soon as tomorrow. A Yule baby for sure. We weren't going to host the ritual today, but I like being around my fellow brothers and sisters."

She kept her eyes closed and started humming. Peter gave me concerned look and I took it as a hint to leave them alone. I planted a kiss on her cheek.

"Congratulations and blessed be," I said. I shook Peter's hand before I left to join the others outside.

The ritual involved a log with some etched symbols representing peace and love. I looked around for Corey, hoping he had slipped in late. I wanted to make sure he was okay after he took off during our last encounter. I didn't see him.

Lenore lead the ritual. Though they didn't join us, references to the life budding in Nasaide's womb were brought up many times. The theme was rebirth. We bade farewell to the sun as it disappeared behind the line of earth in the distance, and burned the log. It was the death of the old sun into the longest night of the year, and the birth of the new sun arriving in the morning.

We celebrated with drinks in the living room and kitchen. Sophia poured despite being in a little pain from her headache. She had a whole line of sweet drinks memorized in red and green colors, mostly of cranberry or sour apple flavors. Not wanting the hangover, I stuck with a simple IPA and sipped quietly in a corner. Despite my frequent visits, I didn't feel connected with many of the others in the group, and with Nasaide and Peter keeping to themselves in the dining room, and Corey missing in action, I began to search for my coat and intended to slip out early.

Just then, Leonore broke out from the dining room.

"Attention everyone! We're about to have a baby!"

Cheers erupted across the home.

"Sadly, we're going to have to end our festivities here. If you don't mind cleaning up after yourselves and showing yourselves out after we leave."

She approached me, "Jacob, my car is a bit cramped and Peter wanted to sit in the backseat with Nasaide. Is there any way I can convince you to drive us to the hospital?"

I tucked my arms into my jacket sleeve, "I wouldn't mind at all. Mind navigating me to the hospital?"

"Of course."

There was some rustling as I got my car from a far parking space and rolled it up to the front of the house. Luckily, my massage table wasn't in the back seat as it usually was. The car shifted with the weight of Nasaide and Peter, and finally Lenore, stuffing her flowing garb into the front seat. I could only imagine what the hospital workers would think of us. Suddenly, we were off.

Peter, who was quiet for most of the evening, lead the charge at the hospital. He had called Nasaide's doctor while we were on our way and took care of the front desk person, who looked like she was on the last hour of her shift. A wheelchair was brought out and Nasaide and Peter were whisked away to the magical delivery lands behind two push doors.

I called June while Lenore and I waited in the seating area.

"Baby?" June asked. She sounded dazed and bored. I could hear the television in the background.

"Yeah, the hosts were expecting and I drove them to the hospital."

"They couldn't find another pagan friend to do that?"

"June…"

"Sorry. I'm just really bored. You and I haven't really done much since you've started going to these events. Now, you're delivering other people's babies. I miss you."

"I asked you if you wanted to come."

"And I told you that I wasn't into that sort of stuff."

I sighed.

"I don't want to fight with you." I said.

"Just... come home when you can, okay?"

"I will."

I hung up, feeling depleted. Lenore sat across from me near a couple with their fussy baby. I had wondered if people would stare at Lenore in her garb, but seeing her sitting down among everyone else, she could very well just be in some exotic style dress. No one paid much attention to her.

"What's wrong dear?" She asked.

"It's June. I don't know if she likes me doing the pagan thing."

"Oh?"

"It's a time problem. She doesn't think I spend enough time with her."

"If you have to take a break from our group meets, no one will blame you."

"Thank you."

An hour ticked by. Lenore made a few phone calls to alert others what was going on. She gave Sophia a call and told her not to worry about coming down, that transportation was provided. It sounded like the gathering at Peter and Nasaide's home had dispersed and Sophia was cleaning up. She was such a good person. After a few agitated silences on Lenore's part, it sounded like Sophia was coming over.

There was a commotion in the back. Someone sounded a color code over the intercom. A few doctors rushed from one section of the hospital to the maternity ward. Lenore, who switched seats during her conversation with Sophia, squeezed my hand.

"I don't like this," she murmured. "I don't like this at all."

For a while there was only muffled commotion.

In a roar of heavy breathing and stomping feet, a bed rushed passed the swinging doors followed by a doctor and Peter. Nasaide was in the bed. She was whimpering and sweaty. There was blood on the sheets.

"My goddess!" Lenore stood up and ran to Peter's side. "What happened?"

Peter seemed confused, his eyes were wide and the color in his face was gone. "We're headed to the emergency wing. I don't know. She was fine and then…. I'll keep you posted." They all disappeared behind another set of doors. I stood patiently on the flat blue carpet of the hall. I could hear a child crying nearby and a hushed voice of the front desk person whispering into a telephone. Sophia walked in just then. She had a smile on her face, but her eyes were winced. I could tell she still had a headache.

"Did I miss anything?" She said happily. Her expression changed when she looked into my eyes.

"They just got moved to the emergency room. Lenore went with them." I knew I said the words, but they felt foreign. I began to feel a cold wave of panic rush from my heart to the ends of my limbs.

Not now. Not here.

"Excuse me," I said.

I walked outside and just stood near the entrance. I knew I was breathing hard. I could see my breath in the wind. I could feel the sweat on my face, heavy and stale. My eyes pulsed with my speeding heart. I felt hot and cold and engulfed and falling all at the same time. I squatted near the brick column, facing the glass doors to the hospital. Sophia was inside watching the double doors. The couple with their now sleeping child sat comfortably in their seats. Everyone feels so distant and unapproachable when I have these attacks. The whole world seems so normal and so right as I feel so crushed and bruised.

"This is fine," I told myself. "You haven't had one of these in a long while. Just breathe. Just breathe."

I put my head between my knees and let the cool air circle me. I could hear footsteps beside me as someone walked passed. *Pay them no mind.* I let the cool air into my belly and imagined it calming me, my feet, my legs, up to my torso, trickling down my arms to fill my hands to my shoulders with relaxation. I felt better. I let this sensation continue up to my head where it peaked at my scalp and overflowed, washing me in comfort. *I am fine. I am fine.* I sat still for a while, not wanting to fall back into panic.

Sophia was talking to Lenore. There were tears in both of their eyes. I could tell Lenore was looking for me and Sophia pointed out the glass doors to where I was seated. Feeling more in control of myself, I stood up and walked back inside.

"We lost him," Lenore said. She choked on emotion. "We lost the baby."

"Where were you," June said as I walked through the front door.

"I told you. I was at the hospital," I dazed across the hardwood floor. I was still thinking about Nasaide and Peter, distraught and in pain. Peter had looked like he'd seen a ghost. Apparently, it was the stillbirth of his son. Sophia told me she had transportation covered and told me to head home.

"I don't understand why they had you drive," she said flatly. Considering the circumstance, it sounded insensitive and cold.

"I'm getting closer to them. I spend time with them. You don't understand what it's like. These people are very united by their pagan interests. It brings us together…" I knew she was looking for something to say, something scathing. I quickly added, "they lost the baby."

June's face froze in shock. The corners of her mouth softened. "I'm sorry, Jacob. I didn't know."

"I know."

"It's just I've been feeling a little neglected. You've been wandering off with these people and you and I haven't done anything for months now."

"These people?"

"Don't turn this into something it isn't. I'm okay with your new identity. I'm okay with you pursuing this stuff, but does this, any of this, include me? Do I fit in your life too?"

"Of course. I've been asking you to come with me for a while now."

She shook her head. "That's not what I'm talking about. Let's do something together. At least once in a while. Maybe once a month? You give them that kind of attention, why not me?"

"Okay. We'll go out. We can see what Sam and Benny are doing, maybe?"

"They want to have us over for New Year's Eve with a few of their other friends."

"Yes, let's do that."

14

June and I celebrated Christmas in our usual way, alone and at home. My brother had the kids in my family so my parents would rather spend time with him in California. June's mother, Carmen, wasn't up for another trip north in the cold. She said it was bad for her arthritis. She did recommend we attend morning Christmas mass, which she does every year. Christmas mass had been a tradition we held for ourselves since we met at the Christian outreach. We never went on Christmas day, but during Christmas Eve we went to the most accessible and convenient mass we could find at Saint Matthew's in the District.

It was strange walking into a tall catholic church building after so much paganism. It wasn't that I felt overwhelmed to repent. Quite the opposite, in fact. Seeing the massive statues with their placards and accompanying murals had me wishing for more paganism. After all, who are the saints, but the avatars of church-shunned pagan gods of the past?

Saint Matthew was a tax collector in the Bible, if I remember correctly. This made him an appropriate saint for the District as the patron saint of civil servants. In front of the red building were stone steps complete with a swearing homeless man at the bottom, demanding the church-goers give him money instead of giving money to the church. The wide wooden doors at the top of the stairs wore Christmas wreaths with red ribbon.

There were more Christmas adornments inside, mainly Douglas fir's and dozens of poinsettias. A nativity scene was set up in one of the wings with a porcelain and blonde baby Jesus stretching in a trough with hungry animals breathing nearby. Shepherds dotted the outskirts with their curious lambs.

June and I sat in the left pews. She listened intently while I dozed into the murals and miniature shrines around us. It was all beautiful. I had forgotten how much I adored cathedrals with their high domed ceilings with painted angels and saints. I wished paganism had something like this, but then, what is nature if not a church for the wild children? What is the sky if not the mural of our many gods?

The choir sang a series of Christmas carols. Their voices echoed across the tall hall as if the angels in the paintings sang back. We left after "Hallelujah."

"Have you ever considered Christianity?" June asked me when we were home. She had melted a brick of Mexican chocolate into some warm milk and we sipped it while staring out the window.

"I was raised Christian, remember?" I admired her. She had her dark brown hair bunned up with a pencil.

She nodded. "I was, too. Catholic. And yet, it's only been tradition to me. Never something I believed in."

"I believed in it. I just stopped at some point. It was gradual. I think I realized I was no longer a Christian after Afghanistan."

"So 'no atheists in foxholes' is a lie?"

I chuckled. "I wasn't atheist. I was just wandering in spirituality. I still am. Being pagan doesn't mean I have any answers. Paganism is a spirituality based on wandering." I wasn't sure if that felt wholly true, at least not for every pagan, but it was true for me and generally true for the pagans I've run across. I let this thought turn in my head for a while as we stared into the misty streets.

"Merry Christmas," I whispered to June.

"Merry Christmas," she whispered back and her free hand reached for mine.

Benny and Samuel had a few friends over to their apartment, in the heart of Washington, DC. Benny, the baker of the two, had an array of different cookies, from thumbprint-jam to gingerbread bells decorated in frosting. They had a decent sized one-bedroom in the Shaw area. The living and dining areas were large enough for the seven total who drank behind their walls.

Benny had called me "the prodigal son" when I stepped through the doorway. I had been distant from the two since my delve into the witch scene. There was another couple in the room: a stocky fellow in a dark green sweater named John and his fiancé, Carol. Carol was a grade-school teacher and spoke like one too, over emphasizing her words as if she were addressing a room full of five year olds. Then, there was Chuck.

Chuck was a heavyset man in his early forties with curly red hair and glasses. His mustache slightly curled near the ends of his lips, giving him a late 1800's gentlemanly appeal. Every time I've seen him, he'd worn a slacks with button up shirts. I'd never seen him wear anything like tee shirts or shorts, even when I've run into him during hot summer months.

"Mr. Ayers," he started with a grandiose bow, "it is a pleasure to be in your presence again."

He took June by the hand and kissed her cheek, "Lady June, beautiful as always."

June blushed, "Thank you, Chuck. It's always good seeing you."

We spent a great deal of the evening listening to Chuck tell his great stories about the places he was able to visit. Chuck worked for the government as many of the DC folks did, just as Sam and Benny did. He was always full of tales about the type of awkward people he'd run across and the few times he would get rip roaring drunk at some fancy socialite gathering where it was considered impolite to get rip roaring drunk at. He was from another time. I always felt like I was listening about some great soiree of an older century when he spoke.

Carol burst in with a few of her strange parent stories. Mostly about parents with either no regard for their children's education or who seemed to blame Carol for every missed school day or late homework assignment. I couldn't do what Carol did: teaching. I was okay with kids from a playful place in my heart, but it always seemed weird hanging out with little kids as an adult.

I mentioned this to the group and Carol raised an eyebrow. "Oh, no! Kids are great! I love children. I want to have four or five of them after John and I get married. Have you two thought about kids?"

"Uh."

"Well," June scratched her neck. "We haven't really discussed all of that."

Carol hid her face into her wine glass. I thought I saw a slight nudge taken from her fiancé.

"My, my, my. This is awkward," Benny said wiping his glasses on his napkin. "I almost feel like making it more awkward…"

"What are you going to…" I started, but Benny finished.

"So tell us about your new found pagan spirituality, Jacob. Sammy has been curious about it since you started."

Samuel turned a light red and cast a glare at his boyfriend.

"Well," I started, "It's going well."

Carol's face lit up. "Paganism sounds fascinating. John ran into some pagans while we were in England, didn't you John?"

John raised his eyebrows.

Carol continued, "They were *Druids*! Can you believe that? Druids!" She gave a mousy little laugh.

"Yes," I said. "Actually the main group I've been hanging out with consists mostly of those who identify as Druids. They're right here in the DC area."

There were a series of "ah's" heard around the table. Samuel leaned forward.

"What does that mean, though?" It was John. "What does it mean when they say they're 'pagan' or even 'Druids?'"

"It's a bit hard to explain. Not even I fully understand all of it and I've been involved for the past five months." I took a breath. I wasn't sure how I was going to begin, so I took a shot at the word "pagan."

I started, "The word 'pagan' is actually the antithesis of the word 'urban.' It was a derogatory word used to describe those in the rural areas who didn't abide by mainstream practices. Of course, now, pagan has been used to describe those who do not believe in the mainstream religions."

"Like Islam, and Christianity, maybe Judaism." It was Samuel. I was surprised by how enthused he appeared.

"Sort of. Paganism is an umbrella term for all of *those* people. So it's really hard to pin-point what each person means when they identify as pagan other than that they see themselves as being apart from mainstream religion, but even that is a gray area. For example, there is such thing as someone who is a Christopagan, a combination of Christian and pagan."

Sam tilted his head. "So a pagan might still subscribe to a mainstream religion but not with the mainstream approach."

"Yes," I said. I took a sip of wine while I figured out what to say next. I wasn't exactly an expert on the matter, but I felt that was understood.

"Within paganism there are many groups. Some of them are Druids, some are Wiccan, some call themselves Heathen or Asatru."

"What does that mean?" It was John again.

"Heathen or Asatru… well, I don't have any experience with them though I know they exist here in private circles. They subscribe to the Old Norse religions."

"Like Odin, Thor, and the World Tree?" Samuel asked.

"Yes. Druids are a group that basis their spirituality on the little we know about Druidry."

"I thought we knew next to nothing about Druidry," John said.

"Yes, that's true. But some believe that what Druids stood for can be found in a few Roman accounts as well as from folklore and myth from the area. They believe that some of the Druid beliefs are hinted at in those stories."

John got quiet. I couldn't tell if he was thinking about what I said or was flat out pissed off at me. I continued either way.

"Wiccans are a group that branch out from the teachings of Gerald Gardner about witchcraft."

"So they're witches?" Carol chimed in.

"Yes, Wiccans are witches but not all witches consider themselves Wiccans."

"Why is that?"

"Well, it's complicated. Some don't resonate with Gardner's work. They think it's watered down and the diet soda version of what it means to be a witch. Some identify with older or what is considered non-Gardnerian witchcraft. Some don't identify with Wicca just to set themselves apart from the rest, it seems. I think there are more in that last category than will admit it."

"So, what? These people cast spells and whatnot?" John asked, aggressively. Carol placed a hand on one of his shoulders.

"They do. It's called witchcraft," I smiled.

"Fascinating," Chuck said. "Just fascinating. How are the people like? Are they spacey?"

I laughed, "Many of them are pretty out there. I won't lie. There are quite a few who seem to think that they have some special gift that no one else is capable of. A lot of puffed up egos. But then, once you learn how to sift through those types, you get a lot of folks who are very sincere and actually quite grounded."

"Fascinating," he said again.

"Well, I'll be honest, it all sounds like a bunch of crock. No offense." It was John again. I could tell that he didn't care if offense was taken or not.

"I'm sure you're not alone in thinking that," I said.

"People acting like they have some sort of power over other people. It's wrong." John continued.

"Oh, don't say that John." Carol said. "Wiccans are nice people. I'm sure they would never curse anyone. Right, Jacob?"

I nodded, but I had to really think about that one. So far I've met some pretty good people, but some pretty emotionally unstable one's as well. What if something set them off? Would they raise their wands and begin smiting?

The conversation shifted to some of Benny's hilarious gossip. I put my hand on June's shoulder. She had been quiet the entire time we talked about paganism. She felt stiff, but calmed down when I massaged her gently as the night went on.

When the time came, we watched the ball drop and brought in the new year with a kiss.

"I love you, June." I whispered as I held her. She whispered an "I love you" back, but it was stifled. It felt forced. She was so stiff and quiet.

"What's wrong?" I asked, knowing I wouldn't get an answer. She shook her head gently and gave me a soft squeeze.

John and Carol left. Carol gave sweet hugs and kisses and John gave tight gripped handshakes. He stared me straight and the eyes and said, "Well, you're weird but good luck to you."

"Have a safe trip home," I responded. The idea of being the 'bigger man' came to mind, but in the end there really is no "bigger man," is there? There is just submission to society's definition of peacekeeping: the neutered "yes man." Feeling defeated, I returned to the table which Benny had cleared plates from, and I had a sip of my remaining wine.

"What an asshole," June said sitting next to me.

"I wasn't sure if anyone else noticed," Samuel said.

"You guys know him well?" I asked.

Sam shook his head, "Benny and I are more friendly with Carol. This is only the second time we've encountered John."

"He is an uptight mess, but I love Carol to death," Benny said. He refreshed our glasses. "Now, June, are you going to go to one of these pagan events and see what they're all about?"

June tightened up. "Well, I…"

"If you really want to know what Jacob does at one of those gatherings, you're going to have to jump into one."

She blushed at this one and I grabbed her hand for support.

She looked at me. "Well, I've been thinking a lot about it and maybe I could go to one."

"There you go," Benny said, "Jacob is there an upcoming gathering you can take June to?"

"Things are pretty quiet next month, but there's Imbolc at the beginning of February."

"What in God's name is an Imbolc?" Benny laughed. We all did. I could feel June calming down.

"It's a celebration of the first signs of spring."

"Signs of spring? In February?"

"Yeah, it doesn't strike me as a favorite."

Benny looked at June and she nodded.

"I guess, that's that," she said. "I will be going with you to Imbolc."

15

Sophia lived in a cottage style house in one of the Virginia suburbs. The house itself was white with brick accents and dark brown breams. There was a chimney that smoked slightly. All around it were barren trees which I'm sure exploded green during the spring time.

The neighborhood was made up of various styles of homes, from full red brick to cerulean stucco. Instead of street lights, each house had a style of street lantern that guarded an accompanying mailbox. It was too cold to see the neighbors, but I knew they were there, probably peeking from the corners of blinds and drapes.

"This is a nice neighborhood," June remarked. She pressed on her full sized coat made of grey wool. She earlier had a hard time picking out what to wear to her first pagan event. I explained to her that I kept it pretty simple with my apparel and she decided on a light pink blouse under a cloud gray sweater, and a red tartan skirt. I told her she looked like a Catholic school girl and she replied with "But I am!" She joked about putting her hair in pigtails, but settled for keeping her curled locks out and down against her neck.

I kissed her.

"What's gotten into you?" She asked.

"I'm just excited for you is all."

"Don't pressure me. I'm nervous as it is."

"No pressure. None at all."

"Can you get the macaroni and cheese?"

I pulled out a large steaming bowl from the back seat of the car.

"You think it'll be enough from the both of us?" She asked.

"Yes. Sophia loves to cook. If anything, us bringing this is going to cause a fuss as to where it's going to fit on the table."

"Okay."

"Yes?"

"Okay, I'm ready. I love you."

"I love you, too."

We approached the house from the driveway and followed a line of concrete path across the lawn near a sign that read "Beware the flying monkeys." June gave a little chuckle but then stopped abruptly. I could tell she felt unsure whether laughing at such a thing would be appropriate.

Lenore answered the door wearing a deep purple cloak and a lavender shawl. She embraced me as soon as she recognized me. I could hear her multitude of trinket necklaces chime against my own brown coat.

"This must be June!" she clapped her hands and held them out for a hug. "It is so good to finally meet you. Jacob has told us so much about you."

"It's a pleasure to meet you as well," June said. She seemed distracted by the rings on Lenore's fingers.

Inside, we were met by Sophia and a huddle of women I barely recognized, though they seemed to know me quite well and were excited to meet June.

"Seeing you two is a breath of fresh air!" One of them said. I think her name was Ally. She had a round face and figure and she smiled a lot.

Corey appeared then, from somewhere below, maybe the basement. I forgot that he lived with Sophia temporarily, though it seemed he had been living with her for quite a while now. I smiled at him.

"It's good to see you, friend." He said with a grin. I saw him eyeing June and realized they had never met before.

"Let me introduce you," I started, but Corey waved his hand.

"No, no. Not yet. The hens aren't done clucking at her."

We stood together in silence and watched. There were the typical wreaths and candles decorated around the room. I had placed the mac and cheese on a table full of other foods, most made by Sophia. There was a giant bowl in the center with a ladle. Sophia filled the bowl with what looked like Mexican hot chocolate from a giant pot. The smell of chocolate, nutmeg, cinnamon and spices filled the room. She winked at me as I watched her. She looked tired.

"Has Sophia been sick?" I asked.

Corey shrugged. "Maybe she's just exhausted from all the cooking?"

I nodded.

I caught a glimpse of Anna, Lenore's partner, standing in the doorway and on the steps to the mezzanine den. She watched June curiously but didn't approach. I waved at her when we met eyes, but she only smiled wryly.

"Is Anna okay?"

"I just live here. I don't know." He sounded defensive, but I let it go.

June approached us now.

"Very nice people," she said and she held out a hand to Corey who looked down at it with an expression of shock. "I'm June, Jacob's girlfriend," June said, as if to clarify her hand out.

"Corey," he shook her hand. "I live here with Sophia."

"Oh, are you related?" June asked, innocently.

"No," Corey shifted against the wall behind him, "she's helping me out through a rough patch."

"That is very nice of her," she glanced over at Sophia who was now moving plates around the table.

"I'm grateful," Corey said flatly, looking at the floor.

June looked concerned but shrugged it off. We mingled with the others. I tried to get into a conversation with Anna, but she was very curt with me, and dismissive. I wondered if I had done something to offend her, but then I don't think we had much interaction before.

She seemed quiet and distant with everyone, sitting alone in the den-slash-ritual room looking out the window. I did like how the winter sunlight played upon her yellow-frosted hair.

The ritual started and we gathered into the den. Sophia and Lenore had set up the altar with a circle of tea lights surrounding a ceramic bowl of white milk. A dozen or so teacups were also set around the table and a dry ladle was placed to the side.

"It's goat's milk," Lenore explained. Sophia stood beside her, rubbing her own temples and wincing at the sunlight. "It's the closest to ewe's milk we can come to since, after all, Imbolc means 'ewe's milk.'"

She explained what we were about to do. There was a cooler of snow from the most recent snow storm. We were to each take a teacup and fill it with the milk as well as, metaphorically, our intention for the coming season. The snow then would go into the bowl and represent the antithesis of our intention as well as the winter that was beginning to wane. After the designated priest and priestess said a few words of meditation, we were to pour our teacups out over the snow to aid in melting it, a symbol of our new intention overcoming its challenge and homage to the upcoming spring.

"Jacob and June, would you do us the honor of reading for the roles of priest and priestess?" Lenore said suddenly.

I nodded and then turned to June. She didn't look as interested as I, but she nodded small and took a nervous step forward.

"I'll be right here with you," I whispered to her.

She didn't look at me and I could tell she was slightly angry, though she hid it well from the others. Lenore handed us our scripts with a smile and we started with a calling of the four directions as well as a call to the goddess and god. June read beautifully, and though she wasn't happy with being a central part of the ritual, she was putting effort into it that was impressive.

Together we told a story to the others about the old woman who ruled the time of winter, the Cailleach, who left the land allowing the mother goddess of spring to return, nursing her newborn sun child. We told of how the spring goddess journeyed through the underworld these past winter months and how she now rose back to the surface of the world to rewarm it.

We performed the milk ritual together. The den was so crowded that I was concerned someone would spill, but no one did. June spent some extra time on placing her intention into her cup and I wondered what she thought about. I caught a glimpse of Corey, eyeing her with a look of concern.

"So mote it be," we said after it was all over.

We ate in the living room on chairs that were pushed to the sides of the room. People raved about our macaroni and cheese and how appropriate it was to eat diary during this time. June sat quietly to the side. She didn't say a word to me, but she appeared cheerful after the ceremony. I wasn't sure if it was an act or not, which meant it probably was. I sat next to her and Corey joined us, making small jokes and trying to get us to laugh.

"You two," Leonore approached us, "Ally was right. You two are a breath of fresh air. This community has had a rough time these past few weeks with the baby and all." Her face suddenly became very grave. "But seeing you two shining brightly at the center of our ritual today brings us so much hope for the future."

June seemed to loosen up at hearing this and her smile felt genuine. "Thank you so much. I'm glad we could be a part of this."

Lenore took her hand between her own and said with tears in her eyes, "Blessed be." Lenore disappeared to the den taking Sophia by the arm. Sophia was still wincing and I felt sorry for her. Corey watched them with that same look of concern on his face.

"Has she been having migraine problems or something?" I asked.

"I think so."

"I'm sure she'll be okay," I said, though I wasn't sure if Corey's concern was actually for Sophia.

"Have you heard from those guys?" Corey asked suddenly.

"What guys?"

"The ones from the party a couple months ago."

"Jason and Gideon? No. I have not."

"Well, maybe they were busy, huh?" He was still looking into the den.

Lenore's voice could be heard slightly above the others, though no one else seemed to pay much attention to her.

"You have a problem, Sophia," she said, "and you need to get rid of it."

Corey shot up at those words suddenly.

"Excuse me," he said, and he headed down to the basement which I assumed was where he was living. We didn't see him again the rest of the evening.

"So what did you think?" I asked June in the car while we drove my silver hatchback toward Arlington. It started snowing and June opted to drive since she didn't trust my Californian instincts, even though she, herself, was from Florida. The snow was anything but harsh. It fell in thick fluffy flakes that danced in the sky before collecting on the sidewalks below.

"It was okay. Not what I expected at all."

"You seemed upset for a bit there."

"I didn't like being put at the center of the... rite? ceremony?"

"The ritual. I'm sorry about that. I was thrown into the center too and it felt awkward to tell them 'no.'"

We made it to the loop of connected highways known as "the beltway." There was hardly any traffic. I suppose many folks avoided driving in the icy weather.

"Was everyone kind to you, at least?" I asked.

"Oh, they were perfect. Everyone was very welcoming. It was a very warm environment, though I don't think that Corey guy liked it there, though."

"Corey? Really?"

"Not at all. He seemed really anxious the entire time, unless that's just how he is."

"Maybe." I actually never thought about it.

"Overall, I enjoyed myself. It's still not my thing. It felt like a prayer group and you know how I feel about that kind of thing."

"I suppose so."

"Does that bother you?"

"Having the group be compared to a prayer group. Yes, it does, actually."

"Why? I thought you wanted to group to be seen as 'normal'"

"I think I wanted to the group to be seen as 'extraordinary.'"

"Well, I'm sorry I don't feel what you feel about it. It is a nice group, either way."

I suppose without the intrigue of fireball magic and the mystery of occult supernatural activity, a prayer group was exactly what we were. Though, it felt like so much more to me and I wanted to see it as something completely different from the Christian religion. A prayer group. I snorted at the thought.

16

The snow continued for a couple more days, but accumulated very little. What started as light fluffy flakes turned to sideways flying pellets and, soon, to a mush of rain and ice. I heard that bad weather at Imbolc meant a short winter. I wouldn't have minded, but I had work and that meant heaving a heavy massage table around Northern Virginia sidewalks and into client homes. I've canceled appointments for bad weather before, but I needed the money. Valentine's Day was just around the corner and I wanted to take June out and show her I still thought of her.

We went to a Brazilian barbecue restaurant in DC's Logan Circle area. June loved it and we talked about life and where we wanted to go with it. June wanted to eventually get a place in the District, closer to work. She said she had been eyeing houses the past few months.

There was no way we could afford it. Not with my current job anyway and I assumed that was implied. Wanting to keep the conversation tranquil, I bit back any objections and just smiled and listened and added a few things of my own I would like: a den and a library to keep my large collection of books.

I left out any mention of a ritual room or the fact that most of my books were about witchcraft. It was actually relieving not to talk about paganism for once.

Things still weren't fine in the pagan world anyway. Nasaide and Peter were still taking a much needed break. Jason Cedar was still out of reach and I was actually starting to worry about him.

I had heard of a spell that involved placing an object in one's hair and thinking about that person and when that object fell out, that person would get into contact. I imagined the spell was intended more for lovers, but the effect was what I was after so I made an attempt a few days later on a free day.

I chose a time when June was at work to spare me any embarrassment. I used a paper clip, hoping that it would fall out rather quickly. It didn't. It hung onto my brown strands like a sober cowboy on a mechanical bull. I considered going for a run but the dark clouds in the sky made me reconsider.

I continued with my day, cleaning the apartment and any other thing that people do to make their days feel productive. I hadn't wanted to go outside with a paperclip in my hair, but I managed to make it to the local supermarket for some milk and a few other things with a beanie on my head, hoping the paperclip would fall out when I took the beanie off. It didn't.

I was getting anxious. Since my interest in witchcraft, I picked up the habit of assuming everything meant something. So when the paper clip wouldn't fall off my head, I considered all sorts of terrible reasons why. Maybe something had happened to Jason after the party? Maybe he was sick or injured very badly? Maybe he was dead?

The paper clip fell off and clanged on the wood floors.

I stared at it, hoping it wasn't some kind of omen and feeling sorry that I let such a thought pass through my mind while a contact spell was in progress. I picked it off the ground and held it with both hands, charging it with Jason's name. Just then, my phone rang.

"Hello?"

"Jacob?"

"Yes."

"Hey, it's Jason Cedar."

"Jason, how are you doing? It's been a long while. I've been trying to get in touch with you."

"Yeah, I know. I was in an accident."

"Damn, are you okay?"

"I am now. I was out in a coma for a couple of weeks, Gideon too."

"What happened?"

"You know how they tell you not to 'block the box' in intersections?"

"Yeah?"

"Don't."

I laughed at this. "So what happens now? Are you alright?"

"My leg is in a cast and I can barely walk around. Gideon has both an arm and a leg patched up. There's some very painful physical therapy on its way, but nothing is permanent. We're expected to recover."

I filled him in on what happened in the community the last few months, about Nasaide and Peter. I told him about Sophia's Imbolc and how she seemed to be in pain.

"Yes," he said, "she's been struggling with migraines the past couple months before my accident."

"I figured as much. Lenore made it sound like there was a specific problem with it. As if something was actually causing them."

There was brief silence on the other end. "That's interesting. I have no idea. Maybe she's over exerting herself?"

"Maybe?"

I told him that it'd be good to see him again when he felt mobile enough and that I hope he felt better. He explained it might be a while but if I wanted to stop by and watch a movie on DVD or something like that, he was game. We hung up.

I heard online that Inner Fire was running a spring equinox gathering, or "Ostara." It was being held at a park in Springfield, twenty minutes away from me. The only contact with Inner Fire that I had was at the social gathering in Chinatown and I wasn't planning on going, but Corey called me and asked, surprising since he seemed to not like the Inner Fire style, which I heard him refer to as "fluffy bunnies" once or twice.

There was a long road that circles the park and the lake, enclosed in trees. The leaves still weren't out yet but the robins and other birds were back and they fluttered from branch to budding branch as I drove myself and Corey through to the uneven asphalt of the park parking lot. There was a small concrete dam that bordered one edge of the lake that overflowed and sent a moving stream into a thicket of trees. I saw some families fishing and having picnics in grassy spots along the creek edge.

"It's a bit crowded here for a public gathering, no?" I asked Corey as we stepped out of the car.

"Inner Fire is big on activism and likes to be in the spotlight. This is exactly like them."

"Do you not like them?"

Corey shrugged, "They're agenda driven, that's all, and dogmatic as hell about it too. Something to keep in mind when you hear their rituals."

We trudged along a path, half paved and half dirt, to a small beach with a gazebo and a closed down concession stand. There were faded canoes roped together, probably waiting for warmer weather. I recognized Cham near the gazebo with a handful of others. Pearl and Cu were there as well, the most colorful person there being Pearl. She wore another set of earrings that looked like they were part mojo bag and part dreamcatcher. Around her neck was a necklace made of rainbow colored beads with a pewter pentacle attached. I wasn't sure if it was another chakra balancing set or if it was for gay pride.

Breezes across the stale water in the lake brought in a musky scent of algae and fish. We heard our names as we approached the beach.

"Corey, we haven't seen you in a long while. Welcome back!" Chamomile greeted. She had the tables nearby decorated in purple and blue. There were bowls of food on one of the tables, mostly hummus and vegetables to pick through. I hadn't brought anything and was hoping it would go unnoticed. I did notice that a lot of the food was labeled "vegan" and "non-vegan" which made me relieved I didn't bring anything that would probably just offend someone or waste my time by going uneaten.

Cu Chulain approached me while I dipped a carrot.

"Have you thought about joining me in the fight?" He asked.

It took a while for me to remember that he had mentioned his interest in fighting the "evils of Congress" with his magic. "I've considered it, but I think I'd rather stick to the mundane method of voting to keep folks in or out of our legislative branch."

He looked sad to hear this. "That's a shame. I really had you pegged for a warrior type."

"I could still be, right? I mean there are other evils in the world other than what is in the House or the Senate, right?"

"The biggest evils are in the House right now, with Republicans in charge. They won't stop until they've given all of our money to 1%."

"I see."

"I hate them so much. Just the smell of them. Filth!"

He was really starting to get heated. I looked around to see if anyone was watching us, but no one was. They must be used to this... or in agreement.

"I didn't know Wicca was so political," I said.

"A real witch is involved in politics and votes Democrat. Otherwise, they're not really a witch at all," he said.

I was turned off from this. Not that I wasn't on the left side of politics, but being told how I should vote and what stance I should take from someone who has dogmatically justified hating the other party seemed contradictory in a religion that was supposed to be open.

I excused myself and sat on an empty bench and just breathed in the air. The smell was stale, as I mentioned before, but there was still something relaxing about it. A mist rolled in from the north and seeped through some of the trails and ghosted the trees.

"What are you up to?" a familiar voice asked.

I turned and it was the round-faced Raven I had met before. She smiled at me and I figured she'd forgiven our first awkward encounter.

"I'm just taking in the environment. It's not every day I get to go out in nature like this. It's empowering"

"You *must* be a witch then," she laughed.

"Druids are big on nature too," I remarked, hoping it didn't come off as dismissive.

"That's true. Are you one? A druid?"

"I hang out with them on full moons. Maybe I am to some extent, but I'm really more interested in witchcraft."

"You're talking about Nasaide and Peter's group. Very tragic what happened to them. I feel so bad for them."

"Yes. Me too."

We watched the fog in silence and listened to the birds until the ritual started.

For the ritual, we stood in a circle in a grassy area by the gazebo. In the center was a small table full of flowers and a statuette of a goddess sitting in a chair with a crescent moon on her brow. Ribbons of Easter colors flowed in all directions attached to anything with a stem except for a silver chalice and a spiraling wand centered in front of the goddess. Someone placed a wreath of baby's breath and lavender on a hook in front of the table.

Corey stood next to me with Raven on my other side. She seemed to really want to talk to me this time around, but I wasn't much in a social mood that day.

Chamomile started the rite with a speech about the world changing and growing for the good of all. There was a bit in her speech about how this was a good time to welcome things back which we lost, to grow new things, and, because it was an equinox, a time for balance. She brought up an issue with equality, for gays and for women. She mentioned how this gathering was supporting that cause of equality and how we will remain in the theme of balance throughout the ceremony.

We held hands while the quarters were called and Raven stepped forward and sang a song which she apparently wrote herself. It was beautifully simple, about a fairy child born at Yule, who laughed spring into existence when he was old enough to understand how to do so. She sang it with a faux Irish accent which added fantasy to the rite.

Chamomile stepped up to the center of the circle after the song. She placed a large pitcher of water on the altar in front of the goddess statuette and said, "The Earth is ready for spring. Many of us have been waiting a while for it." There were chuckles across the circle.

She continued.

"Today, the inequality of day and night is corrected and both the day and the night have reached balance in their tug-o-war of power. In a time of long nights and harsh cold, the wheel of the year has turned and the day has said, 'no more.'

"No more to the situation where a gay couple is not seen as equal to straight couples. No more to a transgendered man or woman being discriminated against in hir workplace for being different. No more to a woman being denied her rightful place as man's equal. No more to glorifying war and romanticizing its fighters, but instead glorify peace and equality for all people regardless of their race, gender, religion, or who they choose to love. No more of animals being cruelly treated for our gain when there are alternatives to their suffering. No more of students being drenched in debt to earn a decent living while the 1% look on and not do a damn thing about it!"

There were nods and sighs of agreement coming from all over the group. I shuffled uncomfortably on my feet.

Chamomile lifted the clear pitcher of water up from the altar and raised it in the air. "In the spirit of Ostara, I ask you, my fellow witches...." she shook her head, "No, I demand of my fellow witches, claim your power and do what real witches do: be heralds of progressive change in our communities. Lead the fight for equality and justice. If you stand with me, raise your hand and empower this pitcher of water with me so we can pour it to the Earth to be in agreement with her balancing energies. Raise your hand with me now."

I raised my hand with the others if only to get the ordeal over with. Despite being in agreement with most of what she said (I definitely wasn't going to go vegan), I felt pressured to agree and I didn't like it. I felt like I was in a Baptist church when I thought I was making it a point to stay away from such an atmosphere.

After a while, Chamomile tipped the pitcher over and poured its contents onto the ground. "So mote it be!" She heralded.

"So mote it be," the rest of the group said.

While driving Corey back to his metro stop, we had a discussion about the ritual.

"I felt like it was required of me to be a Democrat and donate money to some progressive non-profit. It was churchy guilt-tripping and I didn't like it," I said.

"Did you disagree with any of the topics she was talking about?"

"Generally, no, but that's beside the point. What if I had disagreed with them. Let's say a controversial situation in the world takes place that isn't so black and white. Let's say Inner Fire takes a side on that situation and Chamomile 'demands' us to be 'real witches' again. What if I disagreed with her, what then?"

"Just ignore it, I suppose. I would just go along until the ritual was over and then leave as soon as I could," Corey shrugged.

"Exactly. It would become a hostile atmosphere for disagreement. I'd rather learn the spirituality of this and come up with my opinions on the world on my own without someone trying to supersede their dogma all over my spiritual path."

"Congratulations."

"What for?"

"You just ran into some 'white lighters' and you left without punching anyone in the face. I thought for sure the line about the military would have riled you up."

"It did, but I held it in. She oversimplified a complex situation. Naive. All of them. Just so god-damned naive about how the world actually works."

"Let it out"

I laughed, "Dammit, I will!"

We laughed and joked the rest of the way to the metro stop and I forgot about Inner Fire and relaxed.

"Let's go camping," Corey said out of the blue, with the metro stop in sight.

I was hesitant. "Where to? When?"

"Soon. I know a place in West Virginia that's not bad."

"Let me talk to June about it first. Maybe."

Corey got real quiet after I said that.

"Don't worry," I said. "I just want to make sure she's alright with it and she should be. Then I'll go."

I veered my car to the sidewalk and let him out and told him I'd call him soon.

"You better," he laughed and then he headed down into the underbelly of the street.

17

Jason lived in an apartment in Crystal City, a small corner of glass paned buildings just south of the DCA airport. It was a decent sized apartment and I wondered how high up the chain he was at the government job he held.

The apartment was a mix of Ikea furniture and hand-me-down antiques, but they worked well together. He had a few items of clothes littered around the place and there were some discarded food cartons on the sink, but I assumed they were there because of his broken leg. He didn't strike me as a necessarily messy person.

His face was bruised around his left eye with some discoloration on his jaw. He looked different and I wondered how much of that was the accident and how much was my perception changing.

"I had some surgery," he explained. "It was worse a couple weeks ago."

Jason, who was wrestling with Gideon only a few months ago was now much slower paced and fragile. He moved around the apartment carefully. A book edged across a corner on the coffee table gave him trouble and he used one of his crutches to tuck it back properly on the wooden surface.

"Need help?" I asked.

"I'm good," he said. He wore a blue long sleeve waffle shirt and some loose shorts. He swiped at a sock on the sofa and tossed it into a ball in the corner of the room.

He asked about Inner Fire and I told him about the ritual and my conversation with Corey.

"Corey? That guy from the party?" Jason asked.

"Yeah, him. Why?"

Jason shrugged, "Nothing." He took a sip from a coffee mug and wiped his mouth with his sleeve. "That activists stuff is pretty typical in paganism. I'm surprised you haven't run into it sooner."

"It might have turned me off if I ran into it sooner."

"Why? What's wrong with a group of folks standing up for something?"

"Nothing, until you add the 'you must behave this way if you want to be considered a real pagan.' It's dogma. I hated it in Christianity and I hate it in paganism, that's all."

"Did you disagree with any of it?"

"The peace activist stuff seemed a bit much, but otherwise I didn't have a problem with it."

"Then, I don't see what the big deal is. Just ignore them if you don't believe in what they're saying."

"I will probably do that. No more Inner Fire for me."

"That's going to be difficult. They reflect a lot of what the BNP's say on blogs."

"BNP's?"

"Big name pagans."

"Give me a break."

"Oh, yeah. Pagans have their celebrities who pop out blogs like it's their bread and butter."

"I guess I'm thankful I didn't know about this until now," I said.

Jason laughed. "Seriously, they're not that bad. They bring a sense of community and discussion that isn't there otherwise."

"What's wrong with just the ecstasy of paganism and the reverence for nature and magic?"

"Well, it all sort of gets redefined by the BNP's as something more practical."

"Well, that's no fun." I said, petulantly.

Jason laughed again. I could tell that it hurt him a little to do so the way he gripped his sides.

"I want you to consider something, but don't get angry with me, okay?" He said, still smiling.

"Okay," I responded, not sure if I wouldn't be angry with him. I hate being told what to do.

"Take a look at the blogs and the activism and just consider how far paganism would have come without them. Then, consider what they bring to paganism that paganism is better off with."

I started to interrupt but Jason raised a hand gently.

"Now, I'm not saying that it all doesn't have its negative side, as you've pointed out," he said, "but consider that there has to be more to this than just ecstasy and communion with the spirit of nature. Otherwise, it's all just internal stuff that doesn't mean anything to anyone else."

"Why does it have to?"

Jason didn't respond to that. We popped in the movie and talked about other things while it played in the background.

I did take Jason's words to heart, however. I checked out the blogs he had mentioned with some BNP names in mind. Most of them were statements about how a witch should behave and read like daily devotionals. I still agreed with them, but found them annoying. They were authoritative, and even as a prior military man, I couldn't stomach that kind of teaching. At least not from someone I didn't know who I didn't consider my teacher.

I began to question if my animosity toward this topic was more about me and my hatred of authority. Hell, it took a lot of pride swallowing just to be taught by Justin who lived across the country and met me by web camera.

I thought on it more in the quiet of my living room, later. It was raining outside and I found the pattering against the windows relaxing. I kept the lights off and let the gray outside light illuminate the room with dripping shadows.

Maybe it was the defining that was the problem. Up to this point, paganism and witchcraft were sold as something I made my own and practiced my own way. With this added factor, someone else tells me how I should or should not practice, usually in lines with socialism and hippie philosophy. I decided that I would continue with my own definition of the craft; keep it moving, growing, and open. I'd keep my political leanings to myself, even if I agreed with the others. My magic is my own. No one defines it for me no matter how good their intentions are.

Corey called me a week later wanting to solidify our plans for the camping trip. I told him I still hadn't talked to June about it and that I would get back to him soon. I had actually been really busy with work. With the warming weather, massages were in high demand and I found myself lugging my massage table all over northern Virginia. June and I hadn't crossed paths as often during the week as I found myself catering to clients in the late evenings to oblige their work schedules.

"I was thinking of going on a camping trip with Corey next weekend if that's okay," I blurted out over a dinner of frozen burritos. June looked up from her plate. Her expression was blank.

"Oh?" It was flat and cold.

"Yes, just for the weekend. I made a lot of money this week and last to afford taking a weekend off."

"With that Corey guy?"

"Yeah… is there a problem with that?" My tone came off condescending, even though I didn't mean it to come off that way.

"Jacob, what about me? I would have liked to go on a camping trip with you. I hardly see you now as it is."

"We can," I said. "We will. Maybe in June when it gets warmer? You and me and maybe we can invite Sam and Benny…."

"Instead, you're going alone with this Corey guy."

"What's wrong?"

"We don't see each other anymore, Jacob. And the one time you decide to take off from work you want to go on a camping trip with someone else?"

"Do we always have to do things with each other? Is that what this is about?" Again, it came out demeaning and I could see June wince at my words. "That's not what I meant," I said.

"I don't trust, Corey. He was giving me the evil eye the entire time we performed that damn ritual you forced me to go to."

"I didn't force you to go to anything. I asked and you said you would."

She sighed heavily and crossed her arms.

"What is it?" I asked. "Where is this coming from?"

"I just told you! We don't see each other and even when we do, you're preoccupied with all that pagan stuff."

"I thought you were okay with my spiritual stuff."

"I am, but don't forget me. You keep forgetting me. I'm here. I would like to go camping."

"Well, you can come with us."

She scoffed. "You know what? Just go on your trip. It's fine." She stood up and walked to the bedroom and slammed the door.

I followed her to the bedroom and waited behind the door.

"June, if you don't want me to go, I won't go." I called. I heard rustling on the bed.

"God, just go," she said.

I walked away feeling angry. What did I do? I didn't feel like I was ignoring her. This seemed to come out of nowhere. I sat at the table and forked some of my burrito dripping with hot sauce. I took a bite and then reached for my phone. I punched Corey's name on my recent call list and waited.

"Corey," I said when he answered. "I'll go camping with you."

He seemed pleased with this. "That's great news. We'll have fun."

I hung up and sat in the kitchen in silence.

18

We left early the following Friday. The sun wasn't completely up yet and only the morning star shined brightly in the sky. I kissed June lightly on the cheek before I left. She was awake, but she lay in bed with the blankets up to her breasts, staring at the ceiling. She said nothing when I told her I loved her, but called to me before I left the room.

"Have fun. I love you, too."

I picked Corey up at Sophia's house. He was ready with a massive rucksack and a sleeping bag waiting on the outside porch. His red hair was on fire in the morning light. He zipped up a light jacket he wore and stuffed his ruck and his sleeping bag in the backseat next to the cooler and some of my gear.

"You want to do breakfast?" he asked.

I shrugged, "I don't mind if we do."

I drove to a small 24-hour diner located just inside the beltway. It smelled of grease and syrup. Old newspaper clippings were posted on the wall in glass frames. I ordered an omelet with black coffee and Corey inhaled a stack of pancakes with butter. We were quiet, for the most part, both still too tired to hold a conversation.

Afterward, we stepped back into the cool morning air and drove onto the beltway, then to the I-66 highway. Normally, I hated this highway, but it was empty and even if it wasn't, we were leaving DC against the angry commuters who would be driving in on the other side.

It wasn't a long drive, but it was full of contrasts. The busy urban background gave way to suburban strip malls which died out to patches of grass from huge lawns to country houses. The sun was brighter here and the air was fresher. It warmed enough and I opened the windows to let in the scent of green as we passed into the West Virginia line through the Shenandoah. All around us were budding trees with hints of leaves and some with pink and white blossoms.

"I wish the leaves were out fully," Corey said finally. He yawned and rubbed his face.

We arrived at the campsite around 11 and the sun blared down on us in all its near-noon fury.

"It's hot as fuck," I said. "It wasn't this hot in DC."

"Welcome to the wild." Corey said. He stretched his arms over his head and looked around.

The campsite was set on the side of a mountain near a lake. I could smell the water in the air. There were a few people camping alongside us, quietly grazing on sandwiches in the shade of tarp canopies.

It took a couple of trips but we managed to get our stuff to our plot and I began to set up the tent while Corey set up a canopy for us to relax under. I thought of June while I did so. I wished she had come with us.

"What are you thinking about?" Corey asked.

"Nothing."

"You're biting your lip. I noticed that about you. You bite your lip when you're thinking about something."

"Who doesn't?"

"I don't"

After the tent was up, I grabbed some lunch meat from the cooler and ate it plain. A breeze came in and I closed my eyes as the sweat evaporated from my skin.

I heard some rustling as Corey grabbed some bread from a bag and proceeded to make himself a sandwich.

"You want to go for a hike after you eat?" I asked.

He smiled up at me. It was boyish and pleased. "Sure."

We hiked around the lake following a small trail marked with signs. We were hardly off the beaten path, but it was still nature and I felt renewed by it.

"Do you think Inner Fire folks are into the great outdoors?" I asked.

"You really don't like them do you?"

"I'm over my dislike of them. I'm just curious if the city pagans ever get out of the city."

"Some do, I imagine. They're like any other group with their mix of personalities."

We came upon a bank with a clear pool with small rocks on the floor. I kicked off my shoes and stepped into the water. It was freezing cold but I stayed inside, allowing the rippling lake to lap at my ankles.

I closed my eyes and said, "Oh water spirits, great spirit of this place, I honor you." I unscrewed the cap from my bottled water and dribbled a small sip from it into the lake.

There was some splashing behind me and I heard Corey picking his way toward me.

"It's fucking freezing," he said.

He unscrewed his own bottle and poured a libation into the lake. With a shivered voice he said, "Be honored, oh lake, by my offering."

We warmed our feet on a sunny boulder nearby and watched the sunlight dance across the waves.

"I love being a witch," I said.

Corey said nothing for a while, but then asked, "To you, what does being a witch entail?"

I shrugged, "Honestly, I think of a Bible verse."

"A Bible verse? For witchcraft?" Corey started laughing.

"Hear me out. I'm not taking it verbatim either way. It goes, 'I have shown you, O man, what is good and what the Lord requires of you. To act justly, to love mercy, and to walk humbly with your god."

"That's Micah 6:8," Corey said.

"Yes. I'm surprised that you know that."

"It's one of the better verses, though I don't think it fits entirely with witchcraft as it is."

"No. That's why I say, I don't take it verbatim. Witchcraft to me is all about helping the weak and the disadvantaged. It has a sharp edge to it as well. I would say that it is the job of the witch to ensure that justice is played out, having the means through magic. As for walking humbly with god…."

Corey laughed again, "I doubt any witch wants to be told to be humble or submissive with any deity."

"Not at all. I can't speak for everyone, but I was always taught that we are equals with the gods. So I would modify that part of the verse to say something like 'be proud that you are a witch, but be aware that you are not always right' and 'walk with Spirit.'"

"Interesting." Corey said. "That last part, the 'walk with Spirit' part, does it aim to demand a belief in a higher power."

"No," I said. "It only means to be in constant communion with our own power. Without that communion, I don't believe we can do anything magically. Spirit could mean a lot of things to different people. I know there are witches who are also atheists."

"So," I continued, "I think altogether it would go something like: 'Oh, witch, you know in your heart what you must do: Ensure justice, have compassion, be proud, but be honest, and commune with your power.'" I laughed a little at the end of this, feeling foolish.

Corey didn't laugh. He rubbed his drying feet and stared thoughtfully out onto the water. Streaks of reflected light danced across his face.

"What are you lost in thought over?" I asked him.

"Huh?"

"You got real quiet."

He bit his lip, then said, "I don't think I believe in rules about witchcraft."

"Why is that?"

"Well, think about it. Witches are supposed to be on the outskirts of society. They are outside of rules. When you start adding rules and absolute definitions, you create another subculture that needs to be adhered to, that real witches would still be on the outskirts from."

"So 'do what thou wilt?'" I said.

"I guess so. But none of this 'harm ye none' crap. It's impossible to follow."

"Oh yeah?"

"You can't wipe your nose without harming something. It's a just a rede anyway. A rede. Do you know what that means?"

I was going to answer but Corey cut me off.

"It's just advice. Not a damn law," he said, getting heated.

"Okay. Calm down. Any 'laws' or 'rules' anyone comes up with is their own either way. I would like to think witchcraft gives one the power to choose what kind of witch they want to be by constructing their own values."

Corey stood up and nodded. We continued around the lake until we reached a steep slope in the ground dropping directly into the lake. We searched for a way around, and we were sure there ought to be one, but feeling tired we decided to turn around and return to camp the way we came.

There was a family camped not far from our tent, a Hispanic family that shared dark hair and medium brown skin with dark eyes. The father motioned us to come over and he offered us some soup that he made.

"I made too much," he said. His speech was toned with a sliver of an accent. "Albondigas," he said and he pushed a paper bowl forward each to Corey and me.

It was delicious, warm and spicy. I ate mine quickly and the man was fast to refill my bowl. He introduced himself as Antonio, and his wife's name was Sariah. He had two boys, Eddie and Jacob, who played a simple card game over a blanket in the grass.

"Jacob is a good name," I said. "It's mine."

One of the boys looked up at me with passive curiosity, but I could tell he was more interested in his game.

The sun set and Antonio bade us to stay longer while he set up a small camp fire. He was a mechanic from Richmond and his wife stayed at home with the kids. She read from a book, now with a small book light attached to a hard cover. It was an Anne Rice novel.

"You like ghost stories?" I asked her.

"It's not really a ghost story," she said, sweetly. "It's a vampire story, but I suppose there are ghosts in it." She didn't have Antonio's accent. She was beautiful in the fire light and her dark hair curling around her shoulders reminded me of June. I wondered what June was doing in the apartment without me. It made me sad to think of her alone.

"Have you heard of La Llorona?" Antonio asked, suddenly. He had a guitar out and he started strumming. I expected him to start into something Spanish and quick, but he picked his strings to a ballad by Metallica.

"La Llorona? What's that?" Corey asked.

Little Eddie and Jacob appeared close by. They huddled next to their mother.

"She's the crier. She drowned her children and as penance, she roams the world mourning them."

"You're going to scare the boys," Sariah said.

"We're not scared." One of the boys said.

"I've seen her," Antonio continued. "I was about 15 or 16. I was throwing the garbage in the alley when suddenly there was a chill. The wind got very still and the air became thin."

I thought about the time we ran across Stephen Cook's ghost. The air had been thin and still when we experienced him, too. I felt a tingling across my spine, but I tried not to show it while Antonio continued.

"Suddenly, there was a haze of what looked like white smoke pouring over one of the fences at the far end of the alley and a woman walked out of it. She was pale and her clothes didn't match today's clothes. She walked without moving her legs and she got closer to me."

"Were you afraid?" One of the boys asked.

"No, not at first. I felt like I could have been dreaming, but I was awake. My mind couldn't register what I was looking at until she passed by me and I heard the low hum of her moans. I could see fresh tears dripping down her face and her clothes were wet and sloppy against her. It was her eyes that terrified me. They were like human eyes only the way they stared off... as if there was nothing there. As if I wasn't there."

"What did you do," Corey asked.

"As soon as I recognized what I saw as being supernatural, I ran back into the house and told my dad, your grandpa Jose," he turned to his boys.

"What did he say?" One of the boys asked.

"After I told him everything I saw, he laughed and told me I had seen La Llorona! And you know what? He had seen her too when he was younger. You know what that means?"

"What?" The boys asked.

"One day, you will see her too!"

The boys laughed, but it was a nervous laughter.

"You see? Now they're scarred for life." Sariah scolded.

"They'll be okay. As long as La Llorona doesn't take them with her."

We all started laughing then, except the boys. They got real quiet.

That night, Corey and I shared a tent. I didn't think anything of it but there was a sense of longing coming from Corey that I didn't notice was there at first. While I was turned in my sleeping bag, my bare back exposed, I could feel one of his fingers tracing something on my skin. He must have thought I was asleep. I shrugged lazily, and pushed the sleeping bag up over my shoulders.

THE WHEEL AND THE DAY

I could still feel his arm reaching across the tent, just inches from me.

19

"I don't want to be part of Nasaide and Peter's group," Corey said as we drove back along the twisted rural roads on Sunday. It was cooler that day than it was the day we had arrived and we kept the windows down to enjoy the clear weather.

"Why not?" I asked.

"I've outgrown them. I don't need them anymore."

"Is that what it's all about? No sense of community or friendship?"

Corey straightened up. "I just don't feel like I connect with them anymore."

"Is this about the talk they had with you? You're not mad at them about that are you? What happened there?"

"Nothing," Corey snapped. "Just some so-called elders trying to butt in on my business."

"Lenore, too, eh?"

Corey was quiet. He kicked his shoes off and put his bare feet on the dashboard.

"I'm hungry. Are you?" He asked.

"I could eat."

I wanted to question him more about what happened, but I figured I was being pretty nosey about the whole situation and decided to back off. It really was none of my business.

I pulled over to a fast food restaurant in the first real town we reached. When we sat down to eat, I turned my cell phone on and it buzzed with notifications. I checked my voicemail. Sophia's soft voice filled my ear.

"What is it?" Corey asked me.

"It's Sophia. Lenore had a bad seizure and is in the hospital."

Exhausted, I walked through the front door of the apartment and tossed my camping gear aside. June was rinsing off dishes in the sink. She turned her head to the side and mumbled a "hello." It stung. I knew she was still upset with me, but I didn't know what to do about it.

I kissed her on the neck and told her I loved her.

"You stink," she said. "Go shower."

After a warm shower I came out and found my camping gear was tucked back into the closet and my duffle bag with my clothes was disassembled and thrown in the laundry basket. I got dressed and padded barefoot to the living room where June was cozied with a blanket on the couch, staring at the news.

"Thanks for moving my stuff," I said. "I love you."

She nodded, ran her fingers through her hair, and remained quiet. I wanted to kiss her on the mouth and get her to look at me. I wanted to cuddle on the couch right next to her to let her know I still cared. I left her alone. I let her steep in her thoughts, believing that she needed the space and maybe some time.

I went to the spare room and lit a small candle and I prayed to the Goddess in the flickering light. I asked for healing for Lenore and healing for myself and June. I blew the candle out.

Sophia had invited me to a small Beltane celebration at Lenore's house, hosted by Lenore's lover, Anna. I was told that Beltane was typically a day for joyous celebration but due to recent events, it would be a time for healing. I felt fine with this. I needed healing as well.

I parked the car near one of the wooden ranch fences and walked inside Lenore's house. Lenore, of course, was still in the hospital, but Sophia greeted me when I walked in. She wore a beige shirt with leather string zig zagged at her chest. A light linen cloak draped at her shoulders with a leaf shaped clasp holding it to her neck.

"It's been too long," she said, smiling and hugging me. "Did you enjoy your camping trip? I know Corey did. He talked on and on about it and you."

I felt my blood rush to my face. I need to have a talk with Corey about our platonic relationship. "It was a good, relaxed time," I said.

The main room was decorated with boughs of flowers and leafy branches of trees. The people inside were mostly dressed in street clothes, but some were in pagan garb. I found Nasaide and Peter in the crowd and I greeted them heartily.

"Oh it's so good to see you!" Nasaide said. Peter was quiet but smiled at me warmly.

I told them I missed them and that I thought of them often.

"That's so sweet of you to say," Nasaide said, her voice a chime of bells.

I felt suddenly awkward and blushing.

"It's definitely good to see you," I said quickly, and I rushed away into the crowd.

The crowd was full of familiar faces. Raven was there, along with Chamomile and Pearl. There was the other Raven from the Samhain drum circle. I recognized a few folks from Peter and Nasaide's Druid circle and some from Inner Fire. The house was filled and there was next to nowhere to sit. I went outside in the heat of the evening and found some grass to squat on with a soda in hand and waited for the sun to set.

I felt better outside, safer. Although it had been mostly under control, my anxiety was teetering on rupture at this over-crowded party. Not only that, but Lenore's lover, Anna, was eyeing me since I arrived and seemed suspiciously cold.

I wiggled my fingers in the earth and tried to let my worries seep into the ground. The sun was bright orange and edging closer to the tree line that surrounded the property. In the center of the yard stood a short table with pictures of Lenore and of Naisadie and Peter with tea light candles. Flowers were thrown around the altar and one giant white pillar candle sat in the center, unlit. There were torches staked through the lawn and lit in each direction: North, East, South, and West.

"You really like being outside, don't you?" It was Raven from Inner Fire. She peeked out from the back door with Chamomile in tow. They both joined me on the grass. Raven in a black tee shirt and dark jeans, Chamomile in a light skirt that echoed the wind. They both sat cross-legged. Raven sipped on diet soda while Cham had a red cup of something in her hands.

"I needed to get away from the crowd," I said.

"So do we. It's pagan hell in there."

I laughed.

"You guys haven't seen Jason, have you?"

"No," Chamomile said. "He's still hobbling back at home. It'd be too hard for him to get around this group."

"That's true. Feels like he's been in crutches forever."

"He's getting better," she replied. "He'll be on a cane soon."

"Poor guy."

"He's in good spirits." She seemed to want to say something else so I remained quiet to allow her to sort through her thoughts.

"You were in the military, right?" She said, finally.

"Yes, I was."

"Deployed?"

"OEF. Afghanistan. I was a corpsman. It's kind of like a…"

"A medic. Yes. I know what a Navy corpsman is."

"Did Jason, tell you?"

"My cousin was in the Marine Corps. He knows all about Navy corpsman. But, yes, Jason and I talked."

I felt uncomfortable. "Oh, yeah?"

"Yes." She didn't say anything else and I took this as a chance to change the subject.

"So when's the next Inner Fire get-together. I'm surprised you didn't have your own Beltane already planned."

"We had one, but we canceled it. This healing for Lenore and for Nasaide and Peter is much more important."

"Yes," I agreed. "It is."

"You know," she started, "there is a degree of paranoia that takes place when negative things happen at the same time."

"Oh?"

"For instance, Anna thinks that someone brought this type of energy to our community. Maybe even on purpose."

"Who would do a thing like that?"

"That's a good question. Probably no one. But people get irrational when tragedy strikes."

"That explains the weird looks I've been getting from her."

"No one actually believes it was your doing," Raven interjected. "It's just Anna being paranoid, I'm sure."

"Maybe I shouldn't have come." I said.

"No. You're fine here. Obviously Nasaide and Peter have vouched for you. Everyone else wants you here," Raven said.

Chamomile stared at the grass and quietly nodded her head. It was clear that she was thinking of something else.

I felt awkward for most of the night. We gathered in a circle around the table and Sophia lead the group. It was different to see her in the role, but she was a natural. She spoke about the community and told the stories of how Nasaide and Peter started their Druid group. Then she described Lenore as the community's unofficial elder. She lit the tea lights under their pictures and Nasaide and Peter were asked to step into the center of the circle. We raised our hands to them and sent waves of invisible healing energy.

It was palpable and thick. Still, I asked myself: *Is this real?* The ceremony wasn't about my feelings of magical legitimacy, however. It was about sending good vibes to those who were hurting. So I swallowed my doubts and just allowed myself to send the energy to Nasaide and Peter, and distantly to Lenore in a hospital bed in DC.

For that moment, I believed it worked.

Nasaide cried and Peter held her close to himself. They said a few words of thanks and that the Druid group would continue. Nasaide pressed her hands over her belly which was flat and thin and baby-less. I couldn't even imagine the pain. There was applause and a few of the Druid members said some kind things about Peter and Nasaide.

Then Anna stepped up.

She smiled, her wild blond hair fluttered in the wind. She wore a knitted green shawl over an off-white dress. The dress she tied with a cord of what was probably hemp. She told a short story about Lenore; how they met. It was a Beltane gathering in the 80s that brought them together. Lenore was in her mid 30s then and Anna had been 25 and married to a man. Anna struggled with no children that her husband wanted so badly. Anna actually said he "demanded." When they first met in a drunken stupor, lying in the grass of a giant field, Anna told Lenore everything. Lenore kissed her. It was the most gratifying kiss that Anna ever had. Lenore then whispered in her ear, "goddess, grant this woman a child with her love."

Sadly, no child came for Anna and her husband. Her husband left her a few years later and Lenore and Anna grew closer until they fell in love.

"We never had children, obviously, but I would say our relationship was my child and I was glad to nurture and grow it," Anna said. There were tears in her eyes. She looked around the crowd, at all of the faces, and then she reached me and there was a terrible coldness to her expression.

"I ask you all now, as a community, to be on your guard. Ward up. There is some negative energy flowing within our group. Whether it is intentional or whether it is purely the ignorance of a beginner, I can't say. Ward up. Keep your protections on your homes and on your loved ones. Don't think for a second..." She stuttered and covered her face. More tears ran down her cheeks.

Sophia walked out to hug her. There was a moment where we only watched Anna, watched her pain. Some in the circle raised a hand to her sending more healing vibes. I started to raise a hand, but I caught a glimpse of Anna's scowl thrown in my direction. I sheepishly placed my hand back to my side. There was a murmur within the circle and I suddenly realized that I was being talked about. Everyone knew about Anna's feelings toward me. But why? Had I said something to her? Did I do something that would cause her to suspect I had bad intentions?

I felt a hand on my back and it was Nasaide. She whispered in my ear.

"We stand behind you, Jacob. You're always welcome with us." She kissed my cheek and I nodded thanks as Peter put a heavy hand on my shoulder at my side.

The ritual ended with a few words from Sophia regarding the nature of Beltane and what it was about for us, the welcoming of summer. She mentioned more but I was too busy thinking about Anna and her hostility toward me. I thought about sliding out of the gathering after the ritual and heading home, but Nasaide and Peter wanted none of that.

There were drums, like at Samhain. One of the Ravens pounded away at a green bongo drum and people danced around a small fire. I was hesitant at first, but soon I joined them, forgetting my standing with Anna for a while. Soon I was enraptured by the experience. The rhythm of the drum, Nasaide belly dancing nearby, it was an ecstatic dream. Suddenly, couples were shedding their clothes and jumping naked over the fire with cheers from the others. I thought of June.

"I have to go," I told Peter.

"What? Why?" he asked.

"June's at home by herself and I need to be with her."

Peter nodded and I hugged him, then Nasaide. Raven wrapped her chubby arms around my neck and so did Chamomile, though Cham felt rigid and formal. Sophia was nowhere to be seen and I assumed she was inside with Anna and a few of the older members of the group. I thought it best to leave through the side gate and creep around the house to my car.

20

It rained on the way home. I wondered if the pagans at the Beltane gathering packed up their belongings and headed home or if they still danced around the fire, naked and in rapturous joy. I hoped for the later. The idea of dancing in the rain made me smile and wished I was back at Lenore and Anna's backyard with the others, maybe myself naked and wild. That energy of the gathering had me feeling happily anxious and I couldn't wait to get home to June, to share that energy with her. Maybe things would start to change.

I parked the car in our dripping underground garage and headed up to the apartment to find June huddled on the cream colored sofa with a pale pink throw blanket over her legs. She was staring toward the television but it was off and only her reflection returned her gaze on the blank screen.

"Hello, baby." I said, smiling big. I wanted to behave as if everything was okay. I wanted to rewind to the good days when we weren't at odds with each other, the days when I didn't stupidly abandon her on a camping trip. Maybe those days would creep back up and everything would be fine.

She looked at me and nodded. Her eyes were tired pink and her dark hair rested wildly around her head. I closed the door and kneeled at the couch, rubbing her legs. She recoiled slightly and it hurt me; it stung my heart.

I said, "Please, June. Please. I'm not sure what to do to make you happy."

Her eyes hardened and I saw anger on her face.

"You can start by getting a real job," she said flatly.

"We're doing okay with my massage gig. We're not suffering."

"No. No, we're not, but it's too unstable for me," she snapped. Then she said softly, almost to the wall, "everything about you is unstable."

"That's not fair. I'm working on myself. I'm getting so much better. I'm right there. If you'd just let things play out…"

"No."

"Things just need to play out." I said.

"Things don't need to just play out. You need to make some decisions," she said angrily, suddenly pointing her finger at my chest.

"I'm changing. I'm actively changing. I don't know what else to tell you."

She cried, pulling her hands over her head and covered her face. It sounded like a laugh at first.

"You aren't changing. You're just all over the place. You're like a single wheel rolling down the street, following whatever cracks in the street there are, and I keep waiting for the day you spin around and fall flat on your side. We all know it's going to happen. You can't keep doing this to me."

"June, I don't understand. Where is this coming from? You seemed okay just a few months ago. You were supportive just a few months ago."

"Fine. Now, I'm pissed. Now, I'm fed up with all of it. You need to get your life together. It's too rabid and crazy and you're taking me with you and I want some stability." She started sobbing.

I reached for her shoulder and she pulled away. I reached again and this time she gave in and let me touch her. It broke me. It really did.

"Hey," I whispered. "I love you. I'll change for you. I didn't know it was like this for you or I would have changed much sooner. Just give me a chance, okay?"

June didn't respond. She kept her face in her hands and shivered with tears. "I think it might be too late," she said behind her palms.

"Never. It's not too late. We can fix this."

I kissed her forehead. She didn't pull away and this gave me some hope. I kissed her again and again and then I started singing.

"I don't hardly know her, but I think I could love her. Crimson and clover. Over and over...."

She dropped her hands to her lap.

"I'm sorry," she said.

"Why are you sorry? You have nothing to be sorry about. You felt ignored and you felt that I was taking you along for a ride. I should be the one who's sorry. I'm sorry." I kissed her on the cheek, and then I reached for her face with my hand and guided her lips to mine.

I was kissing her, and then she kissed me back.

"Come on," I said, and I guided her by the hand down the hallway and into the bedroom. It began with a kiss. She cooed as I rubbed her shoulders and nibbled on her neck. She remained stiff at first but she softened and soon she was reaching for my pants.

Sex with June that night, was the most primal and wild sex I'd ever had with her. I carried with me the essence of the fire dancing pagan in my sex; the wild ecstasy of Beltane. We were both fueled by it. With every thrust and moan we were the god and goddess of heathen lore, in the wild fields and jungles, making love to honor all things, all life, every poison, and every death. We were the creators of existence and June was my goddess. She would always be the goddess to me.

When we climaxed. My god... when we climaxed, and she was on top of me, her slender body turned beautifully in the lights from the window. Her breasts. Her belly. The ripples of her sex. Orgasm is the tableau of Divinity. We created galaxies in our love.

We fell asleep tangled together with the blankets on the floor. I slept hard and I dreamed I was a stag coming into a clearing of grass. There were witches there dressed in ancient furs with bone beaded jewelry, sitting around an egg. It was hatching. As it jumped and jiggled one of the witches approached me. It was Nasaide, still pregnant with her dead child.

"Magic can change things in an instant," she said.

With my stag horns I nodded at her, but she looked at me gravely and, as if I didn't understand the first time, she said, "Magic can destroy everything in a moment."

I woke up.

I was alone.

"June," I called out. There was no answer.

Thinking nothing of it, I stretched and kicked the sheets off my naked body. I threw on a pair of fresh underwear from the dresser, noticing that June's clothes were not on the ground where mine were.

"June?" I called out again. Nothing. "She must be in the restroom," I said out loud. Then, I noticed the other drawers of the dresser, June's drawers, were hanging open just enough for me to see that they were empty.

I tried not to panic. "June? Please…" I stepped out into the hallway and noticed the bathroom door was open and the bathroom sat empty. June's toiletries were gone. Vanished. I turned the corner and checked the kitchen, hoping that I would find her standing at the oven, frying some eggs or buttering toast, but the toaster oven was clear and the oven was off. No June smiled at me from behind the kitchen counter. There was no June sitting at the dining room table or cuddled with the throw blanket in her spot on the couch.

It was when I peered into the living room that I saw it. A note written in blue ink lay flat against the coffee table.

"Jake," it read, "I can't even begin to imagine what is going through your mind. It seemed for a moment that things were back to the way they were, but I can't do this. I can't pretend that things are going to get better when I know deep down that they are not. I'm sorry to leave you this way, but I love you too much to leave with you standing there watching me. I am going back to my mother's. She and I have been talking about this for a while and I had already bought the plane ticket. I'm sorry. I'll arrange for the remainder of my things later. Good luck to you, Jacob. —June.

I sat down on the couch. Outside it was sunny and clear, I could see from the windows. Chipper sunlight warmed the faux wood floors. The weather mocked me. Inside I felt cold and empty. Tears ran down my cheeks but I ignored them.

She was gone.

"But she didn't give me a chance," I mumbled quietly. Birds laughed outside. I could only sit perfectly still.

21

I watched the time tick by from the mess of my bed. The comforter lay scrunched on the ground since the day she left me. My phone rang incessantly. There was a time that I jumped at the chance to check it, to see if she called me or texted me. It was always a client or a telemarketer who somehow reached my cell phone number through some service I signed up for. Once or twice, Jason called me but I ignored him. I didn't have the heart to tell him what happened or why it happened. I was embarrassed. Humiliated. Broken.

I hardly ate. I couldn't remember sleeping. If I slept, my dreams were of lying there in bed, watching the sunlight reflect off the ceiling in slants from the blinds. Time had no meaning to me. Before I knew it, it was several days passed and I knew I had to at least try to work. I had rent to pay. I would need to buy food. So, I scrounged up enough courage to check my phone.

I'm sorry, I would say to my various clients. I've taken some time off, but I'm available now. Would you like to set an appointment?

They loved me. Told me I was the best in the area and that they waited for me to contact them instead of seeking out another therapist. I was pleased. Really, I was. But I had little energy and massage required so much.

She wasn't there to talk to about this kind of thing, which was even harder. I couldn't cuddle with her and kiss her, which often made the day seem so much better. I was tempted to call Benny and see if she contacted him, but I thought better of it. It wouldn't be a good idea to put Sam or Benny in the middle of the break up.

I checked my voicemails. Most were more clients and potential clients. I called them back, and for a few minutes, I felt okay and productive.

Jason left a message, "Hey man, it's been a while. Give me a call and let's hang out again."

I didn't call him. I still felt too wounded to talk about it.

I gave massages and that was about it. My clients' therapy became my therapy. I was painting sadness with my hands and their bodies were my canvases.

"That was beautiful," they'd tell me, "the best of your massages yet."

I painted in blues and cool colors, an army of blue people reflecting my sadness. They loved being blue and purple and turquoise green. Only one of them commented on my demeanor.

"Are you okay?" she asked. "You seem somber."

Yes. I was somber. "I'm fine," I answered back, admiring her eggplant colored skin. "Did you enjoy your massage?"

"It was superb. You really have a way with your hands."

She enjoyed her new coat.

Corey called me. It was a warm Saturday and I was sitting mostly naked in the living room, as I had been doing all week. I stared at the buzzing device in my hand, the sounds of the city outside ruining my inner silence.

I answered it. I don't know why.

"Hello." I said.

"Jake, it's Corey. Are you free? There's a movie playing."

"Free as a bird."

"What's wrong?"

"Why would anything be wrong?"

"You sound morbidly depressed. Is everything okay?"

"You said you wanted to see a movie?"

"Yeah, a horror flick. Come check it out with me, yeah?"

"Okay."

We met at Potomac Yard. There's a strip mall there with a movie theater tucked in the back. Corey borrowed Sophia's car.

"My god," he said when he saw me. "You…"

"Look like shit?"

"…look like you haven't slept in a while."

"I've had a hard time sleeping lately."

He looked like he wanted to say more, but he didn't. We went to the theater and bought our tickets.

"Where do you like to sit?" he asked me.

"I don't care."

"I see."

The movie was a cheesy ghost flick about a house that was haunted, terrifying a New England family. It wasn't anything new. There were a few shock and scare scenes, but for the most part I stayed slouched in my seat thinking about June and how I could get her back. I already tried calling her about a dozen or so times, but she didn't answer and there was no knowing if she actually checked my messages or just deleted them.

I considered using magic. I thought about casting some sort of spell in her direction to get her to answer me, maybe the spell with the paper clip I had done with Jason. I was afraid to. After all, what was the warning that Nasaide gave me? "Magic can destroy everything in a moment?" Was I being punished for magic usage? Was I experiencing some kind of magical backlash for dabbling? Were the Christians right? I felt myself getting angry thinking about it. I wasn't even entirely sure I believed in magic anymore. It seemed so contrived and convoluted. Everything that had happened up to this point really could be contributed to coincidence after all. It was all just a bit of fun, wasn't it?

I suddenly felt foolish for all of my pagan soul searching. I felt silly for ever waving a wand around and for all those times I spent focusing my breathing and sending out my intention. No wonder June left me. I was too silly for her.

"Are you okay?" I heard Corey ask me in a hushed tone.

I hesitated.

"I don't think I believe in magic anymore," I said. "I don't think it's real."

The movie ended and Corey and I decided to meet up at a diner that was on the strip. It was a shitty yellow place with washed generic artwork and stale blue carpet. We sat in a booth in the center.

"So what's this about you not believing in magic?" Corey asked me.

"I just don't think it's real anymore. It feels silly right now."

"What happened?"

The waiter arrived and we ordered food. I opted for a small salad with hot tea. Corey picked a burger and a shake. As thin as he was, he ate like a pig.

"June left me," I said softly after the waiter left.

I couldn't tell if the look on Corey's face was empathy or something else. In the harsh fluorescent light, it actually looked unsurprised.

"I'm sorry, Jacob. That must be really hard for you," he said.

"Yeah. It hasn't been pleasant."

He stared down at his hands, clearly not knowing what to say next. Then, for some reason, I decided to continue, "Things were rough for a while, but it seemed like she was willing to work through it. It all happened so suddenly. She was suddenly unhappy with my delve into witchcraft, then she was unhappy with me, and then she was just gone."

I felt tears welling in my eyes. I stopped talking and just focused on not crying. I didn't want to appear weak, though I was weak. I was wounded and terrified.

Corey said something, but I was too busy concentrating on getting a hold of my emotions to hear him.

"What?" I asked.

"Is this why you don't believe in magic?"

I shrugged, "I'm not sure. I may have always not believed it existed."

"What about when we saw Stephen Cook's ghost?"

"Is that magic?"

Corey looked away and heaved a sigh.

"It's some evidence that there is more to reality than what we can see," he said.

"But we didn't actually see the ghost. We just heard some bumps and footsteps. For all we know there was a squatter."

Corey frowned. He didn't say anything else about magic the rest of the night. I complained more about June leaving and how I wished she was back. Corey listened quietly and offered small advice on getting over her. This made me angry to no end. I didn't want to get over her. I wanted her back! I held my tongue. I knew he was just trying to help.

My weekly check-in was due for Feri that night, so I excused myself.

"I'm here for you," Corey said, hopefully.

I waved a goodbye and left.

At home, I stared at a blank page on my word processing program. The cursor flashed at me to write something, but I couldn't think of what to say to my Feri instructor. I started off listing the exercises I worked on that week and the number of times I worked on them. The answer to this was zero. I was too busy this week, sulking.

Finally, I typed.

"This week was rough. June left me and I'm not sure if I blame my dabbling in magic or not. I don't think I can Kala this away. Sorry for the short check in."

I copied what I'd written to a discussion board on the Feri website and submitted. It was short but it was honest. I wasn't sure what Justin would say to it.

The next day I got a text message from Justin.

"Are you okay? Let's do a video chat."

I had nothing better planned so I agreed to it. I slunk to my computer desk and set up my webcam.

"How are you doing, Jacob?" Justin said when he appeared on screen. He wore a light green tee shirt that highlighted his dusty hair. He had lost weight since I'd seen him last.

"Justin. It's been a while."

"Indeed it has. Why don't you tell me what's been going on?"

I told him everything: starting from June and Imbolc and our ritual positions there, then I told him about the camping trip and how I knew June didn't want me to go but I went anyway. Justin winced at this. I didn't blame him. It was a stupid decision. I told him how she seemed indifferent to my spiritual practices at first, but then somehow became irritated by them.

"It was like a light switch went off," I explained.

"I understand," he said. "She may very well have been holding in those feelings the entire time and couldn't hold them in any longer."

Those words stung. Of course, I had considered it, but hearing it from someone else made the possibility seem that much more likely. I tried to respond to this but I choked, and then I started crying.

"I'm sorry," I muttered, "I just feel so helpless."

"Have you thought of using magic to bring light to this topic? Maybe some divination?"

"I have drawn some tarot cards on it."

"What happened?"

"The Tower, Death, the three of swords, even The Hanged Man. All cards of change or restraint. Something doesn't feel right about this."

"You're right. How are your wards?"

"No, I mean about magic. I feel like I screwed things up by playing in this field, you know?"

"Is that how you view it? As 'playing?'"

"Sorry. It's just that it all seems so foolish now. All of these daily exercises and expecting good things to happen to you because you will them to."

"That's not what magic is about, Jacob. That was never what it was about."

"Well, what is it about then?" I said angrily.

Justin took a deep breath, "Magic is about harmony with the natural forces of nature, knowing when to act and when to yield. That's not to say that we don't have our own will, but our will is only part of the greater energy of the universe."

"What does all that mean though?"

"It means shit happens, even to witches. But because we're witches, or warlocks, or magicians or whatever, we are able to ride the energy of unfortunate events to make them positive."

"I don't know if I have the energy to ride anything. I just want June back right now. There's nothing else I want more. I'd give it all up for her if I knew it would bring her back."

Justin frowned. "I understand how you feel. I've been there. I know that there is nothing I can say that will ease that feeling right now."

"I think I just need some kind of a break. You know? I need to get my bearing back."

"That's understandable."

"I'm sorry."

"No. No. Don't apologize. This constant appeal to self-improvement that this course offers, it can be much sometimes. Sometimes we need a break from it. I get that. Just promise me that you'll call if you need anything else. I'm here for you. The weekly check-ins are optional during breaks, but I would very much like to hear from you. Take all the time you need and let me know when you're up for doing more Feri work."

"I will," I said.

We said our goodbyes and I closed my laptop.

After a quick prayer to the Star Goddess, I pulled a card from my tarot deck in the guest room. It was The Hermit.

"Fitting," I said.

22

Corey proved to be a bigger friend than I realized. When I didn't answer my phone, he showed up to my apartment ready to dig me out of the imprint I made in the couch.

"She left you near a month ago. It's time to get off your ass!"

"It's June," I said.

"What about her?"

"No, I mean it's June 1st. This is her favorite month."

"God!"

"I just paid rent by myself. I don't have much money to do stuff."

"We'll do the Smithsonian's then."

"Fine."

We started out for the metro station and rode the blue line to the Smithsonian museums. I've been to them a dozen or so times. All of them beautiful and unique. Natural history was always my favorite. From the decayed mummies, the dinosaur bones, to the Hope Diamond, I loved it all.

"Let's go to Natural History," I told Corey.

"Sure."

From the front entrance, there is a massive foyer with a statue of an elephant with a raised trunk guarding the other wings of the museum. Corey was very interested in checking out the stones and rocks in the geology section. I agreed and we went up and saw the meteorites and the giant quartz ball.

"Can you imagine having this crystal ball?" Corey said.

"What would the significance be?"

"Trance work and scrying. You could see the dead in that ball."

I looked into the quartz, "All I see is everyone upside down."

"No, Jake. With your third eye. Use your second sight."

"My *second* sight with my *third* eye?" I laughed.

"Oh," Corey scoffed and we headed to another chamber to view the Hope Diamond.

It was on a slate blue holder that spun around slowly inside an acrylic case. The room was crowded and Corey and I only got a secondary glimpse at the diamond from behind some kids. The museum was full of children, all wearing a designated brightly colored shirt announcing their school. They were obnoxiously loud and in the way.

"Check out this cat's eye." Corey said pointing me to a lemon stone with a vertical beam of white light.

"It's pretty."

"It's very protective against the evil eye and also gives wealth to the one who owns it."

"Interesting."

Corey knew a lot about various stones. Citrine, for example is good for mental alertness. He went on to explain that a lot of citrine sold in occult stores wasn't natural citrine, but irradiated quartz to give it a yellow look. I was in awe at his knowledge, though some of it I already knew from skimming through my resource book on magical stones back home.

We wandered the various halls of the Smithsonian, checking out the sea animal exhibit, the exhibit with goat bones, and finally the mummies. I liked the mummies, not for the view of decayed bodies, but because of the descriptions of strange burial rites explained by some of the signs. I was fascinated by the deities and the significance of various artifacts.

We stopped for lunch after checking out the dinosaurs, heading to the basement level for the cafeteria. It was expensive, but I'm sure that food was how the museum gathered a good chunk of their money.

"Do you still not believe in magic?" Corey asked when we sat down.

"It's still being considered," I said.

"Well at least there's that. I was worried you completely given up on me."

"I'd still be your friend even if I didn't believe in magic, I just wouldn't subscribe to witchcraft anymore."

This seemed to make Corey very happy. He beamed at me with slightly red cheeks. I chuckled, uncomfortably.

"What type of magic have you done so far?" he asked.

"A few spells here or there, mostly for money."

"And they worked?"

"I got money when I needed it."

"Well?"

"Well, what? That doesn't make magic real. It could have just been a coincidence. Nothing mind blowing happened when I've cast my spells. Just a few…" I trailed off.

"A few what?"

"Nothing. Sometimes I think I really do see small flashes of lights, like fireflies, but I never know if that's anything or nothing."

"Magic shows itself in different forms to everyone I think."

"Maybe. Maybe not. I admit I could just be upset about June."

Corey groaned at the mention of her name and I laughed.

I continued, "It was a big deal to me. My world fell apart."

"And now?"

"Now, I'm in purgatory. I don't know where I am. I feel blank."

"Do you have a daily practice?"

"Just what I've done in Feri. Some exercises that mostly involve either purifying oneself through Kala, or garnering energy with Blue Fire. There's a lot of meditation involved, too."

Corey scrunched his nose.

"It's really deep stuff," I explained, "It can even be intense. Kala has gotten me out of a few panicky situations."

That's what my anxiety was called now: "panicky situations."

I considered I haven't had a good panic attack for a while now, a thought that was both relieving and worrisome. Sometimes that meant that a big one was on its way. I hoped not.

We continued through the museum, talking about nothing and enjoying each other's company.

There were many days like that. Corey would come unannounced to my place, either borrowing Sophia's car or somehow managing the Northern Virginia bus lines until he reached my apartment in Pentagon City. We would see movies or tour the monuments. Sometimes we would just walk the Pentagon mall and shoot the shit. Soon, I forgot about waiting on June and my calls to her cell phone, which happened weekly and usually under the influence, dropped to nothing.

We were becoming close friends, Corey and I. We were damn near an item, the way he looked at me and took up my time. The way he seemed to get jealous when I mentioned Jason and how I needed to call him and see how he was doing. The way he rested his head on my shoulders during a movie, and I let him, seeing nothing wrong with a little affection.

Corey wanted more and I knew this, but I needed him. He made me stable. He kept me productive. He made me forget. He filled a void in my life that I was reminded of each time I went to bed alone beneath cold sheets, wishing someone would join me. Anyone could join me.

Soon he was grabbing for my hand while walking outside in warm June nights. I shied away, feeling it was too much. I was ashamed on some level by the amount of satisfaction he gave me so soon after June left me. Never mind that it contradicted my sexuality. Or did it?

"Look, the fireflies are out!" I said.

Tiny specks of light fluttered like sparks above a campfire, rising and falling with the wind. They hovered in a grassy area in the park a block or so away from the apartment. Corey tried to catch a picture with his phone but the images kept coming out blurry. At one point he almost tripped and I caught his hand and lifted him up and when it came time to let go, I didn't. I held his small hand into mine and we stood in the darkness of the park with only the car lights shining behind us from passing vehicles. We pretended to watch the fireflies, our breathing shallow and anxious.

I invited him up to the apartment. He had taken the bus that day and I would need to give him a ride home. I offered coffee, as I would have done with anyone. He accepted and soon we were sitting on the couch, laughing nervously at small talk. It was like every other time we had met, only there was something else in the room with us, someone was making the air thin and the lighting dim.

"I'm nervous," I admitted.

He placed a hand on my leg and rubbed my knee with his thumb. Silence. The room was quiet save for a mechanical clock on the light stand in the corner.

"There's nothing to be nervous about," he whispered.

I felt a jolt of fear, as if I walked a ledge of a tall building. I stood up.

"What's the matter?" Corey said, suddenly alarmed.

"Nothing, it's just getting late…"

Then, he kissed me. His lips were soft with just a hint of stubble adding a roughness to my mouth, that wasn't entirely unpleasant. I hesitated at first, but then kissed him back. There were butterflies in my stomach. I crossed an invisible line. I jumped off some unseen cliff. I took it a step further and embraced him, running my hands across his shoulders, then to the small of his back where I pulled him closer to me.

The room spun with his kisses and soon we were in the doorway to the bedroom, pulling at each other's clothes until we were both naked by the bed. He kissed my chest and I ran my lips over his neck taking small bites over his smooth skin. Everything about him was tender and pink and yet strong and unyielding, a blend of masculine and feminine that I had never experienced.

He lay nimbly on his back, his head resting on a mess of sheets. And then I was inside of him, feeling his body from another perspective, tasting him from another fountain. We moved together in a dance of lines and curves. My heartbeat throbbed at his panting and we wrapped each other with our arms until we finished, him moaning in short light breathes in my ear as I bit softly on his shoulder.

"Wow," he said.

I laughed and kissed him. I wanted him more, but there would be time. That night, he slept in my arms with our naked bodies close beneath the blankets. I dotted a few kisses on him as he snored lightly. His thick rimmed glasses sat on the nightstand, illuminated by the moonlight. I thought to myself, how wonderful would it be if Corey were mine. It never occurred to me how much the presence of another man could feel this good. I never considered I would be in love with someone of my own sex, and yet there was a nagging voice telling me in my head that I wasn't in love. I was in mourning. Very well, I thought. I shall take it slow.

23

I woke up alone in bed. Immediately, I panicked. I jumped out from under the sheets and wrestled with my underwear before calling out. I found Corey in the kitchen, smiling in his briefs with eggs sizzling on a pan.

"Good morning," he said.

I was out of breath. I nodded.

"I hope you don't mind," he tapped the pan. "You were snoring this morning and I thought it wouldn't be a big deal."

"No, I don't mind at all. I just thought you left."

"Why would I leave?"

I smiled at him, walked behind the counter and hugged him from behind, placing my forehead on his neck. It felt good to have this kind of connection with someone again. The alarms in my head screamed "take it slow!" I wasn't interested in slow. I wanted to run in at full speed and see where it took me. True, I did not love Corey, at least not in the way that I loved June, but I wanted to. I wanted to feel love again.

"How are you cooking bare chested? Aren't you getting burned?" I asked him.

"I'm fine. I'm good at dodging the splatter."

"You ninja."

I was out of salt and pepper, but I had plenty of hot sauce and tortillas, so we dined on spicy breakfast burritos in the darkened dining area next to the blinded windows. We cuddled some more on the couch before Corey said he had to leave.

"Are you coming to the midsummer gathering on Saturday?"

He asked me.

"What day is it today?"

"It's Thursday. The gathering is at Sophia's place again."

"Sure, I guess so."

I was sad to see him go. I wanted him to stay forever in my arms, skin on skin, smothering him in kisses. But I understood. He kissed me softly on the lips and then headed out dressed in a dark green tee shirt and a pair of khaki cargo shorts. It was the most colorful thing I've seen him wear and yet he seemed so much more colorful to me now.

I cleaned up after he left, washing a pile of dirty dishes and a stack of dirty laundry. The place was a mess and I was embarrassed thinking about what he thought of it all. It wasn't until I reached the living room that I realized that he left his backpack in a chair near the couch.

It sat zipped open revealing a water bottle, a black book, and a folder with paper inside. I don't know what absent state of mind I was to grab the bag by the top handle and pull it toward myself. I know I wanted to move it next to the door, get it out of the way. The contents spilled out over the wood floor: pencils and pens, scraps of paper, some paper clips, highlighters, as well as the black book and his folder. I rushed to pick it all up, worried that I broke something, even though there really was nothing to break.

I gathered his pens and paper clips, his folder, his highlighters. I looked around for his black book, but it wasn't out on the floor. After getting on my hands and knees, I found it under the sofa. It was open when I pulled it out.

I froze, suddenly. What I saw on that open page shocked me. It was a journal entry of sorts, dated late last November. There was a recipe described halfway down the page and the title of the recipe read, "To punish Nasaide and Peter."

"No," I said aloud. I thought about that night with Lenore at the hospital. Nasaide's tears and Peter's anguished face. I read the journal entry:

Last full moon, they cornered me. They demeaned me in front of the other elders of the community. They said I lacked responsibility and that I was mooching off Sophia's good intentions. I have been good up until now but I feel like I deserve some justice here. They don't know my life or my situation with my Dad and why I can't go back. They don't know what it's like. They don't understand what I go through.

The ingredients to the spell included many different herbs, some I recognized as poisonous. There was also a stolen pacifier from Nasaide and Peter's natal belongings. It was very involved as far as the timing went: the phase of the moon, the sign it was in, the time of day, and so forth. I shuddered.

"Corey, what have you done?"

I couldn't believe it. I didn't believe it. He was just here and sweet and loving. How could he do anything like this? Not that I believed it, right? This was just a coincidence. Magic wasn't real. Was it? On that thought I turned the page.

It was titled simply "Sophia." The journal entry whined about things like chores and responsibilities being placed on him. It described how Sophia allegedly demeaned him. How she treated him like a poor dog while he was suffering. I rolled my eyes at how dramatic the entry was. He used a hair pin of Sophia's for this spell, intending to cause her pain every time she thought of bossing Corey around.

I shook my head in disbelief and turned to the next page. This one called "to teach Lenore her place." I tossed the book on the ground.

"This is impossible," I said aloud. "There is no such thing as magic." I was sweating coldly and I felt suddenly very tired. Was it the book? Was there some kind of spell on the book to keep people from reading it? I thought to myself. No. I've only read something unsettling and it's putting me into a type of anxious fit.

"Yes, that's it," I said. "there's no such thing as magic. There is nothing to get upset ab…"

The black book was opened to yet another page as if something wanted me to read it. This one was titled "to get rid of June."

I snatched it up quickly and read the entire page:

I realize now that I can never have love in my life without fighting for it. I decided that I love someone too much to watch him suffer through a relationship he wasn't meant for. She doesn't deserve him and he can do better. I'm simply helping him out.

The arrogance! How presumptuous! He used the scripts we read from at Imbolc to cast his spell claiming that our energy was very present due to the ritual work we took part in. My script had a special use which I found out on the next page.

I've cast my spell on Jacob Ayers, calling him to myself as friend and lover. I don't believe magic can bring about true love, but it can set the stage for it. I burned his script and placed the ashes in a concoction of oils I made. I traced the symbol of Venus on his back while he slept using that oil, and then drew it on my chest where my heart is. I'm sure it will work now that I've gotten rid of his other distractions.

Distractions? I thought of Gideon and Jason. There was no page for them but I wondered. Maybe I was getting paranoid. The stupid book was pissing me off. I thought of ripping it apart, but cooled off enough to consider keeping it intact. I closed it.

Was I wrong about magic? Was it actually real and I was merely in denial about the experiences I've had? Did this book prove that or did I want to throw it out to coincidence again? I found that it was magic I was more inclined to believe rather than coincidence.

I had to tell Sophia, Nasaide, Peter, and even Anna of what was in this book. Yet, I felt stupid about it. What if they didn't believe me? The conversation with Nasaide and Peter would have opened old wounds for them. It would definitely be an awkwardly fragile topic to discuss. Anna would be tough to get a hold of, if she wanted to hear me out to begin with. Then, there was Sophia. I would tell Sophia. She would know exactly what to do and how to handle it.

There was a knock at the door. I put the book inside the backpack and answered. It was Corey, smiling and very much excited to see me again. He immediately kissed me and for some awful reason, I let him.

"What's wrong?" he asked me.

"I have a small stomach ache."

He seemed to buy it.

"What's up? You came back," I said, warding off tension in my demeanor.

"I borrowed Sophia's car. I forgot something," he said. He walked over to the chair and collected his backpack, zipping it shut and fixing the straps against his shoulders.

"Yes, I saw that just a second ago." I wanted to rip his arms off and beat him with them. I thought of June, my beautiful June, loving me just a few months ago, until Corey got his intentions into her. But did that mean I believed in magic? Did that mean I now accepted that it was all real and that it even affected me?

"I suppose, so," I said out loud.

"What?"

"Nothing. Do you have everything?"

"I do." he leaned in for a kiss, but I turned away.

"I might be sick," I said.

"Ah, that's considerate. I love that about you."

I wanted to pull out the black book out of his bag and demand answers. I wanted to punch him in the face and make his nose bleed. I had to consider, however, that if he was a strong enough witch to put Lenore in the hospital, what could he do to me? No, I must deal with this quietly and discreetly. I needed secrecy. This would require magic to counter and I found myself wondering if I had enough experience to take him on myself.

"By the way," he started, "tomorrow we're cleaning up the house and getting it ready for the crowd. Would you be up for helping out?"

"I don't see why not."

Corey left, smiling and excited. He looked me in the eyes.

"I'm looking forward to seeing you tomorrow," he said.

"Me too."

THE WHEEL AND THE DAY

I closed the door behind him, deep in thought.

24

I was ready.

The next morning, after some planning, I steeped myself into a hot bath of salt water which I magically infused with blue fire. I imagined all of the negativity that Corey had drawn on to me, washing away into the tub and disappearing down the drain. It was a simple purification spell. Afterward, I knew I would also do some Kala as well as some meditation. It was exhausting thinking about.

I'm often told that exhaustion is a sign of improper grounding and using one's own energy source for magic, but I had to consider the type of muck that was adhered to me and the amount of time it would take to feel that I was cleansed from it. I felt free afterward. I felt good. There was still some more work to do later that night so I meditated on garnering power from the space around me. I felt less tired and more empowered. My skin was tingling with magic.

Later, I drove to Sophia's. With Corey around it would be difficult to talk with her but I wanted to see what opportunities arrived. Corey answered the door.

"Hey, babe," he greeted me, wearing a white tee shirt and sandals.

I pushed back my anger into a toothy grin. "Hey."

"Come on in."

He gave me a hug when I stepped in and I was grateful it wasn't a kiss. Inside, the place smelled of pine cleaner. Sophia was wiping down the counters in the kitchen.

"Hello, there Jacob!" She called, it felt good to see her again.

"I'm here to help you get ready for Midsummer tomorrow," I

called back.

"Wonderful! Grab a duster, the living room needs it."

Every surface of the living room had some kind of ceramic knick-knack, a statuette, or a fancy stone. I had to move quite a bit to dust off the surfaces. When I finished, I took one of her rugs outside to the balcony and beat it with a short broom. All the while, I kept a lookout for opportunities to talk with her about Corey. How to do that, I wasn't sure. Corey worked a little too close to her for me to just chime in with a 30 second elevator speech about how he was plotting against her, how he put Lenore in the hospital, and how he cursed poor Nasaide and Peter. No, I needed a good hour to go over this with her without Corey's interference or possible retaliation. As silly as it seemed, even to my own mind, I was going with the notion that magic was very real and we were all in danger unless we warded against a very malignant threat.

My next chore was mowing the lawn in the backyard while Corey weeded the garden. The heat was sweltering and soon I was drenched in sweat. When all was done, the yard did look pretty nice. Even the house had a nice gleam to it.

"I have lunch and cold lemonade for you boys," Sophia called from the porch. She had a platter of sandwiches and giant pitcher set out under the awning. She didn't join us, but she watched us from behind the sliding glass door, waiting for us to finish.

"It's hot, huh?" Corey said after some silence.

"Yes, it is."

"I was hoping you'd take your shirt off for me, give me a view."

I grimaced.

"What's wrong?" he asked.

"Nothing. I guess I'm a little shy."

"It's cute." He said it so genially, a bead of sweat dripping down one lens of his glasses. I would have found it adorable in any other circumstance.

A calm breeze rolled across the yard, cooling off my sweaty shirt. I closed my eyes and thought of June. Would she come back after all this cleansing and my plan was enacted? Would I be given a second chance?

I helped bring in the pitcher of lemonade and stored it in the fridge. In the kitchen, Sophia was flipping through a faded yellow cookbook. The book cover paper was scratched and white on the corners. She pointed to a washed photo of candied yams.

"These will disappear at the potluck tomorrow," she said, beaming. "It's a good recipe. I change a few ingredients though but that's a secret." She winked.

She placed an ugly pink bookmark with a beaded tail into the page and said, "It'll have to wait until after I get back from Richmond."

"You're going to Richmond?" I said, suddenly alarmed. How would I have a chance to talk to her now? I didn't want to wait another day.

"Yes," Sophia said, confused. "I'm going to visit my mother. I'll be back late tonight."

"Drive safe," I said.

She placed the yellow cookbook on a bookshelf near the microwave in a line of other cookbooks, equally faded and tattered. She gave me a hug despite my sweaty shirt and left.

"Well," Corey said, "it's just us." He licked his lips and placed a hand on my chest.

"I'm gross and sweaty," I protested.

"We can take care of that."

He led me down to the basement where he had a room made out for him with an attached bathroom. The bed was actually a futon with a pile of sheets, blankets and pillows in the center. Books on witchcraft littered the floor with dirty socks and journals. An idea came to me. What if Sophia came across Corey's journal on her own?

"Ignore the mess," he said. I should really clean up.

"It's fine," I said absently. I looked around for his backpack. It was in a sad heap near his dresser.

"I'm going to take a shower. You want to join me?" He got really close to me.

"I'm weird about sharing showers. There's never enough space, you know? Besides, I don't have clean clothes to change into." I smiled at him, feeling like I accomplished something clever. He looked annoyed.

"Hey," I continued. "Go ahead and take a shower. I'll be out here waiting for you." With that, I kissed him lightly on the mouth.

He moved into me and we embraced. I could smell his body, his sweat, the faint scent of deodorant. It sickened me to be this close to him. He began undressing, grabbed a towel from a nearby cupboard and disappeared into the bathroom.

I darted for his backpack as soon as I heard the shower water start. It was empty.

"Dammit," I hissed. I looked around the floor. There were so many books to rummage through, I didn't know if I had the time. I checked them, one by one. When I didn't find it there, I checked under the futon and inside the mess on his bed. I even opened his dresser drawers. I heard the water turn off and the sound of Corey toweling off.

Feeling defeated I sat down on his mattress and shook my head. Then, I saw it. It just barely peeked out from behind his nightstand, against the wall. I mad dashed for it, pulling it out and ran up the stairs. I made it to the kitchen and quickly pulled Sophia's yellow cookbook from its place on the shelf. It immediately opened to the page with the candied yams. I could hear Corey walking up the stairs from the basement.

"Jacob?" He called.

I pulled the ugly pink bookmark from the cookbook and stuffed it into the Corey's black book on the page titled "to punish Nasaide and Peter." It felt like the most appalling of the spells to stumble upon. I had enough time to push the books onto Sophia's bookshelf before Corey stepped around the corner.

"What are you doing?" He asked me.

I reached for my glass still on the counter from earlier, then opened the fridge.

"I'm just getting some more lemonade. I was thirsty."

I noticed his black book on the shelf. It was sticking out, definitely longer than the other books on the shelf. I moved to the other side of the kitchen to keep his attention from it.

"I think I'm going to head home," I said. "Working outside in the sun has given me a headache."

Corey looked crushed. "But we have some headache medicine here and you can cuddle with me until it gets better."

"I would, but I feel gross and clammy. I think it's best if I headed home." I kissed him on the forehead and rubbed his shoulder, hoping that would be enough. Being so intimate with him repulsed me. He wanted more, though. He leaned into me, biding me to hold him and I did.

"Are you sure there is nothing wrong?" he whispered.

"It's just a headache from the sun. That's all."

He kissed my lips and to keep him satisfied, I kissed him back. I left him, wrapped in a towel in the doorway of Sophia's house. He waved meekly at me and I waved and smiled back before getting into my car and heading home. There was magic to be done and I needed to get ready for it.

At home I took another salt bath, this time with an infusion of mugwort, lavender, and few drops of Crown of Success oil. I wanted to be purified, but I also wanted to be charged with power and connected to Spirit.

I watched the collection of herbs gather near my legs and on my skin. It would take a shower to get the wet herbs fully off my body, but for now I imagined their spiritual essence seeping into me and slow dripping through my skin to my very soul. I heaved a sigh and washed myself of the day's sweat and grief, all the while I thought of June and wondered if she still felt anything for me despite Corey's spell to get rid of her.

There would be time to cleanse her of Corey's influence in a moment. For now, I was to bathe in the purity of the magical water and let my mind strengthen and my power wax. It wasn't the exact day of Midsummer, but I felt the thinning of the veil that was so often described in my pagan books. Midsummer, sometimes called Litha, the height of the sun, was a time for power and working with the spirits of the other side. I was relying on that considering what I was going to do next.

After drying off and changing into some comfortable shorts, I walked into the guest room. I had moved the furniture out to the sides of the wooden floors and against the walls. It was late evening and orange light flooded in from the windows.

I used chairs from the dining area, arranged in a row with white jar candles sitting at their center. There was one for Peter and Nasaide, one for Lenore, one for Sophia, and one for June. I took the liberty of downloading their pictures from social media and I had printed out these pictures of them and taped them to the glass of the candles. On a stool in the center of the room sat a stool with a medium sized cauldron with a small amount of isopropyl alcohol inside for fire. There was a picture of Corey ready beside it. Another stool stood beside that with a single black candle.

I was nervous. Setting up the materials I had felt that arranging them had begun a chain reaction that enabled energy to pulse within the room. I could feel it. I was a part of it. It was the calm before the storm, the static in the air with the foreboding black mass in the distance.

I breathed in deep, allowing my mind to reset itself, to pay attention. I breathed into my soul, the center of my feelings and intuition. Finally, I breathed into my higher self, the part of me that is connected to the Divine. I felt aligned and grounded and ready. With that, I lit my black candle and said my prayer.

"Holy Mother, in you we live, move, and have our being. From you all things emerge and unto you all things return." I bowed graciously to the candle, imagining it contained at its wick, the first spark of life, the light of all creation. It lit up the entire room as the sun faded the windows.

I walked to the East wall of the room, drew a pentagram with my finger and imagined a yellow road leading out from the center of my room to the cliffs of some mountain. I appealed to the spirits of the element of air, asking for their aid. I did the same in the west, to the elementals of water, imagining that same road extending through my room and to a western shore where the undines dove from coral encrusted rocks. I pictured a second road extending to the deserts of the fiery south and breaching my room to the cold earthen north.

"I stand as the guardian of the crossroads," I said aloud. "I stand at the twilight of the realms, at the connection of spaces, at the hem of the veil. I stand between the worlds, the focus of all the worlds."

I tapped my foot, feeling magical energy running across the roads I just drew, and feeling my place sitting at the hub of power. It was palpable. The air tingled with electricity. I no longer carried the doubt I did before. There was too much at stake here. I experienced too much to be skeptical now. The magic in the room was as real as I was, echoing across the world and connecting all life force and egregores, all objects of nature and even those outside of it.

I focused my attention to the white candles, calling upon the spiritual guardians of Peter, Nasaide, Lenore, Sophia, and June, asking them for permission to do my work and asking for aid in healing. It was strenuous work and I felt myself getting light headed asking for each set of guardians for each individual. I lit each white candle as I felt the guardians present and lending their blessing. I grounded a bit before proceeding, feeling the present blue fire licking my spirit and recharging me.

The cleansing ritual was simple. It involved mostly prayer and distance energy healing, sending magical energy to the person subject. I did this with the aid of individual guardians, feeling their presence most fully at the sound of the person's name. I saw them as lights hovering over the pictures on the candles. Giving their light to first Nasaide and Peter, then to Lenore, Sophia, and finally to June. The room was bright with candle flames. I cried softly when I reached June.

"Please," I begged, "Give me another chance."

Then, came the next part of my spell. I lit the alcohol in the cauldron and raised my hands to it, empowering the flames with cleansing vigor. I traced a banishing pentagram over Corey's picture and tossed it into the flames.

"You have no power over us," I chanted. "You have no power over us."

I stamped my feet on the floor, feeling that this was somehow giving more energy to my spell, swaying from side to side.

"You have no power over us."

I thought of the night Nasaide lost her baby. Of the emotional torment she and Peter went through.

"You have no power over us."

I thought of Lenore and Sophia, both kind and loving people cursed without reason by Corey.

"You have no power over us."

I thought of June, sitting in the living room, asking me to cuddle with her, to love her, to cherish her. I thought of her smile and her eyes, her hair and her body.

"You have no power over us."

I was dancing suddenly, taken up by the crackling magic. I was no longer in my guest room. I was in a field and there was a bonfire. I was dancing to the gods of old on a hilltop drenched in grasses and flowers. A star-brilliant sky moved above me, twinkling its acknowledgement of my work. All around me dark trees swayed to my moving limbs.

Then it was over. The fire died down. I was returned to the guest room of my Arlington apartment. I took in a deep breath of grounding energy, being sure to expel the last of my intention to the world. It was done.

"So mote it be."

I thanked the spirits I summoned forth and blew out my candles, saving the black one for last after I recited my Star Goddess prayer one more time.

"So mote it be," I said again, and I flipped on the lights, feeling tingling and powerful.

"That felt like it was successful," said a voice behind me. "How do you feel?" It was Justin. I had my laptop set up in a corner with the webcam on. Justin had offered to lend me some of his own energy during the spell.

"I feel good. I feel accomplished," I said.

"Now that cleansing and protection are in place, you should have no problem addressing the community directly about your concerns."

"I'll make the call tomorrow morning."

I told him about my small stunt, mixing Corey's black book with Sophia's cookbook. It was late and at any moment, Sophia would be home. Whether she was going to work on the yams tonight or wait till tomorrow morning, I was unsure. For all I knew, Corey found his book and was currently plotting against me. I felt safer about this now after my spell. I wasn't worried at all. Regardless, I fully planned on calling Nasaide and Peter the next morning.

"Thank you," I said. "For everything."

25

I woke up early the next morning, still tingling with excitement. I wanted to know how my spell worked, if it did at all, but it was still early to call anyone. I showered, shaved, dressed and headed down to the plaza for some iced coffee and a newspaper. I still preferred a newspaper over internet news. I loved the way the paper smelled and the crackling sound of the pages as I folded through them.

The news was typical. A man was assaulted on the Metro late Friday night. No one was arrested or caught. A senator made a stink about the President. People cast their opinions on gay rights. An uncomfortable noise sounded from the Middle East. I shifted nervously in my seat. I checked my phone. There were no calls.

I decided to go for a walk. The weather was perfect for it. It was eight o'clock and the summer sun was already out and shining furiously over concrete walkways and asphalt streets. The rest of the world was lazily waking. I picked my way around the shopping plaza, slowly, checking my phone every few minutes to see how much time had passed. I told myself that 10 o'clock was an appropriate time to call someone in the morning, but it wasn't coming fast enough.

After a few laps around the block, I headed back upstairs and lay down. Thoughts of Corey swarmed my mind. I wondered if he found the book or if Sophia got to it first. I pictured Corey finding it, mouth agape in shock. He would immediately know it was me who put it there. He'd probably run downstairs to figure out what to do magically to counter it only to find his spells felt flat and powerless. I smiled at this.

My phone rang and I jumped at the sound. I answered it without checking to see who it was.

"Hello?"

"Jacob?"

"Yes."

"It's Peter. I hope it's not too early for you."

"Peter, hello. No, I've been up for a while. What's going on?"

"Sophia found the book, Jacob."

"I see. I'm sorry."

"No, it's alright. Nasaide and I are alright. We were wondering if you could come by for some brunch so we can talk about this."

"Yes," I said, "What time would you like me to come over?"

"As soon as you can. We're just sitting here with Sophia. Anna is already on her way with Lenore."

"Lenore is okay?"

"She's better."

"I'll be right there."

I arrived at Peter and Nasaide's home thirty minutes later. It had been several months since I'd been there. Walking to their door was like a dream taking me back to the days when I first delved into paganism. I even checked the bushes for fireflies. There were none.

Sophia answered the door. Her face was very grave.

"Come in Jacob," she said. She made no offer to hug me as she normally has done and this worried me.

When I walked into the kitchen to join the others, I was met with different facial expressions. Peter looked like he was fighting back some anger. Nasiade looked sad. Her eyes were smudged and red. Anna didn't look at me. She stared at the ground and walls of the room, but Lenore eyed me curiously. She looked tired but her eyes remained sharp. There was a single plate on the kitchen counter with a sandwich and a glass of iced tea. I had the impression that these were for me, but I dared not touch them.

"Jacob, why don't you have a seat," Peter said. His voice was calm and collected despite his angry facial expression. I took relief in knowing that the anger wasn't directed at me.

I sat down on a stool at the counter, in front of the sandwich. There was silence for a moment. All of their eyes were on me.

"I'm sure you are all wondering what happened?" I said, breaking the quiet.

Each motioned their approval. I laughed nervously.

I started, telling them first about June's break up with me and then about how Corey seemed to be immediately there for me. I mentioned briefly that we had gotten close. That's how I said it, "gotten close." They seemed to understand but kept quiet, hanging on my every word.

"He left his book bag at my apartment and I accidently spilled its contents when I moved it. The black book opened immediately to the page about Nasaide and Peter."

Nasaide turned to Peter's shoulder and hung there for a while, hiding her face.

"I didn't believe what I was reading. I hardly believed in magic at the time and Corey didn't strike me as a vindictive individual. ...or maybe he did, but I ignored it, giving him the benefit of the doubt.

"I kept reading that black book and it described awful spells cast on Lenore and Sophia and finally on myself and June."

I stopped there. I felt tears well up in my eyes at the mention of her name. I retained my composure, pushing back the tears.

"What did you do next?" Lenore asked quietly.

"Corey came back and gathered his things. I didn't know how to react to someone who apparently has the power to break up relationships and put people in the hospital, so I didn't say anything until I got a hold of one of you guys in person. This didn't seem like something to say over the phone and it also felt like something I would need proof of."

"So you left the book for Sophia to find?" Peter asked.

I nodded. "I knew I was headed to Sophia's to help her clean-up for the celebration today. I made every attempt to talk with her, but it was awkward, you know? I couldn't just blurt it out with Corey there. I knew she would need time to process it and then there was the proof, which I didn't have."

I told them about how Sophia left and Corey was anxious for me to stick around. I mentioned Corey taking a shower and me finding the book in time to grab it and hide it among Sophia's cookbooks for her to find. I also told them about my spell I cast for healing and protection from Corey, just in case he found the book.

"Thank you for that," Sophia said.

I nodded again. "The plan was to, either way, call one of you today and tell you all about it in case Corey found the book first."

There was silence again.

"Well," Peter started, "I for one am glad you found this book. I think it explains much about what has been going on in our community. Even though you took a roundabout way of letting us know about it, I can understand why you did. I'm actually… embarrassed… that he was able to magically interfere with my and Nasaide's lives so easily."

"It's truly embarrassing to us all," Lenore said. "We should have all been much more warded against these types of workings. Quite frankly, I'm baffled that he was able to cast these spells so successfully. This isn't normal in witchcraft, Jacob. I hope these events haven't turned you off to our spiritual paths."

"Quite the opposite," I said. "Since that spell I performed last night, I've felt more empowered to fight against magic like what Corey has been wielding."

"A natural magical warrior, then." She said. Peter nodded at this.

I smiled, proudly.

"So what happens, now?" I asked.

"Corey has been dealt with this morning," Sophia broke in. "I told him to pack his things and make arrangements to live somewhere else."

"Where he will go?"

"Don't worry about him," Sophia said. "He has an uncle that lives in West Virginia. He's heading over now to pick him up."

"Good riddance," Peter said.

"The Midsummer gathering has been canceled due to recent events," Lenore said. "We're all about to head to Sophia's to do a cleansing and to be with Sophia while Corey waits for his uncle to pick him up. We would be honored if you joined us."

"Of course," I said.

At Sophia's, Corey hid in the basement while we arrived. His stuff was already outside on the lawn, just a few boxes and a couple of bags of clothes. The house ticked quietly to an old clock that hung on the wall in the living room.

We started in the kitchen. Sophia held a bundle of smoking sage she wafted to the corners of the home. Lenore held a stone of hematite. She said it would absorb negativity. Anna held a singing bowl which she circled with a wooden spool. Nasaide held a bowl of salt water which she splashed here and there while we trailed around the house. Peter held a lit candle in a jar. I held a wand and was instructed to fire spirit energy into the corners of the rooms while we walked around.

It was a somber affair. Lenore hummed quietly with the singing bowl held by her partner. Soon Nasaide joined in and suddenly we were all humming to some song we had never heard before. It was a healing experience. We cleansed the second floor rooms, bathrooms, the living room, dining area, and the den. We crowded the den and hovered around the opening to the basement. It hung open like the cave to some monster.

Lenore continued humming while Sophia disappeared into its depths, bringing back with her, Corey, who looked skinnier and paler than ever before. His eyes were bright red behind his thick rimmed glasses. His brilliant red hair looked dull in the light. He looked at us as one would look at the sun, quickly looking back down to the ground before heading outside to wait beside his things.

I heard Peter mumble something under his breath.

We headed down into the dark basement, following the grassy scent of Sophia's sage. We continued the humming and the bowl singing. Downstairs the futon was folded back into a couch. The furniture lay bare and quiet. I glanced beside nightstand where I found the black book, and it was empty. The room was a skeleton of what it once was. We did a walk around, being sure to really spend some time in the corners and in the spaces between furniture, feeling Corey's energy being vacuumed out.

We finished.

Upstairs we sat around the dining table with a bowl of sliced fruit shared between us.

"That was much needed," Anna said. It was the first thing she said all day. She looked at me and smiled warmly. It wasn't an apology for the way she treated me, but it was something and I took it gladly.

"Any other cleansings we should do?" Sophia asked.

"I don't think so," said Lenore. "I feel in combination with Jacob's spell casting last night, this cleansing was really all that we needed."

"Jacob?" Sophia called, "I was wondering if you could do me an uncomfortable favor and give a glass of lemonade to Corey outside. He's a monster, but I'm not the kind to have someone fall over from heat exhaustion in my front yard."

I nodded, though I felt a turning in my gut.

Sophia poured a glass and I walked outside. It wasn't as hot as it looked, but still hot enough to sweat under. I walked slowly to Corey who had his back toward me, sitting on a box. He caught my shadow before I reached him.

"I'm not a monster, you know." He said. His voice quivered. "All of you in there are acting like I left some kind of residue on the walls."

"Here," I said. "Sophia thought you might want this." I handed the glass to him but he didn't take it.

"Please just take it. I don't really want to be out here with you now."

He flinched and his back breathed as if he was crying.

I placed the glass down in the grass and was about to turn to leave when he said, "Everything I did was in self-defense. I was protecting myself from their judgment. You don't see it now because you're in their good graces. I'm sure you think of yourself as the hero in this, but I know you better than you think. You're an individual, not like those types with their sense of community."

"You say that as if it's a bad thing."

"It is a bad thing. You either conform to their communal mentality or you live on the outskirts, never quite fitting in, always fighting to meet their approval."

"Oh, just shut up."

"And June."

"What about June?" I snapped.

"She wouldn't have left you if she already didn't want to. I did you a favor."

"You did yourself a favor."

He got quiet then. He picked up the glass of lemonade and took a long gulp. A rusty red pick-up truck arrived then and parked in front of the house. A gray bearded man who I assumed was his uncle waved to Corey and Corey waved back. Neither spoke to me while they loaded the truck. Then Corey got inside the passenger's side, without a wave or a goodbye. They drove off from the street and turned a corner, and out of my sight.

26

Life continued after Corey. I worked my ass off with my clients, trying to make rent by myself. Sophia mentioned that her headaches had all gone away when Corey left. She thanked me profusely. Lenore seemed to recover nicely from her stroke and, although having no plans to try for another baby, Nasaide and Peter seemed happier and relieved.

Jason called me shortly after Sophia's house cleansing. I was quick to answer this time realizing that if I had only answered his call before Corey got a hold of me, things might have ended differently. He wanted to meet for lunch and I agreed.

"Where have you been?" He said when I met him. He was out of his cast, but used a cane to walk around.

"I've been around. Look at you out of your cast."

"Yes, indeed. I use a cane now, which you can see. But the doctor says I really don't need it. It's psychological she says. Whatever."

"Whatever helps, I guess."

"So tell me, what have you been up to?"

I sighed but I told him everything, starting from Gideon's house warming party. I told him about the camping trip and how Corey traced that symbol on my back. I mentioned how June left me suddenly and how distraught I had been. Then, I went into how Corey was suddenly there for me, how I found his black book, how I smuggled his book into Sophia's cookbooks. Jason listened very intently. He seemed most interested in the spell I cast and asked a few questions about it, like how I came up with the idea to summon the guardians of those involved, and why I chose a crossroads instead of a circle to cast.

"Most of it came to me intuitively. Some of it came from scraps I may have heard or read from the internet."

"I see," Jason said. "I wish you would have called me. I would have been glad to help you get rid of that little bitch. You think he was somehow responsible for mine and Gideon's car accident?"

"It wasn't in his book, but who knows."

"That little bitch," he said again.

Jason rubbed his temples. "Actually that reminds me," he said. "There are two things I wanted to ask you about. First things first. A job opened up where I work and I wanted to know if you were interested. It's not glamorous but it pays decently and you'll have a government job to work at."

"That's great! Yes, I'm interested!" I said. Having suffered to pay rent on my own the past few months, I was tired of the instability of massage therapy. I was hoping another opportunity would show up.

"Great! I'll email you the link you need to apply to. It'd be awesome if we worked together."

I smiled, "It would be. What's the second thing you wanted to ask me?"

"Okay," he licked his lips, "I know how you feel like a badass taking on Corey by yourself…"

"Well I had help from Justin…"

"Let me finish!"

"Sorry."

"Imagine working with others when working magic toward a common goal, how much more powerful would spells be?"

"I'm listening."

"Gideon and I wanted to start a coven and we both would be happy to have you."

"Wow. I actually never thought about joining a coven. Who else is in it?"

"It's just Gideon and me, hopefully you…"

"I'm inclined to jump in and say 'yes,' but let me think about it for a bit. A lot has happened these last few weeks."

"Of course. I totally understand." He smiled, but I could tell he was nervous.

I ended up applying for that job and with the prospects of the job I took it upon myself to get help for my anxiety with the Veteran's Affairs office. They were helpful giving me coping advice as well as medication for the more extreme situations. I didn't feel fixed but I felt managed and that was an improvement.

I didn't hear back about the job until mid-July, and I started a week later. I was just happy to have a steady job. I gave a formal announcement to my clients that I was no longer offering massages and I got straight to work, making a great deal more than I had been making.

The office was a large unmarked building in the financial district. I worked at a front desk for some important bureaucrat, working in data entry while I answered phones and greeted visitors. Jason worked in my office, of course, and we'd go to lunch at the small delis footed into the buildings' ground floors.

It felt good to have what I would typically call a 'grown up' job. I felt more mature and stable. Maybe June was right in asking me to find one. I got sad thinking about this. If only she could see me now. I thought about her often. It seemed the other subjects of Corey's curses thrived after the incident, but I still didn't have my June. I missed her.

I got some disheartening news one day while walking the crowded lunchtime sidewalks. I ran into Benny at a lunch truck at one of the squares.

"Well, well," he said. "Look who looks all respectable."

I wore nothing exciting. I had on a pair of dark blue slacks with a generic button up shirt. It was the most dressed up Benny had seen me though. I hugged him. I was really glad to see him, if just a little embarrassed that it had been so long.

"Sam has been asking about you," he said, "but he's too shy to pick up the phone to call you."

"I've been out of touch too. I could have called." I said.

"We're all guilty. But it's good to see you, honey."

"Likewise."

"Actually, I was meaning to get in touch with you anyway. I don't know how to tell you this, but I'm supposed to collect the rest of June's things and get them to her."

I almost choked. "Yes. I imagine she wants her stuff back." I hesitated. "How is she doing?"

Benny shrugged. "She won't talk about the break up with me. She just says that it's all for the best. She also wanted me to deliver a message to you."

I felt a hint of anger. She wouldn't take my calls but she could relay a message through one of our mutual friends. "What message is that?"

"She says to let her go. Move on. She wishes you the best."

"Oh." I said.

27

I suppose Benny's news could have been worse. She could have cursed me through his lips with all of her mother's vehement hatred of me. Ah, Carmen. I had almost forgotten about her. What conversations took place between June and Carmen, I could imagine. With Carmen whispering in her ear, it was no wonder I hadn't heard back from June.

I was quite proud of myself. Despite what Benny said, I didn't fall apart like I would have if I heard the information just a few weeks beforehand. I was a new man now. I had stability and control. My job performance hadn't fallen. I didn't seek personal days off to sulk on my couch. Rather than hold it all to myself, I actually talked about it with Jason.

"That's rough, my friend," he said. "How are you holding up?"

"I think I'm going to be okay." I responded, and I was.

I still hadn't given him my answer on joining his coven and he was patient enough not to ask me for a response. My magical workings were solitary and done in the comfort of my guest room in the dark with only my Star Goddess candle to light my meditations. I focused on stability and structure as my mantra and within the element of earth. I was a rock and I enjoyed where my personal practice took me.

Lughnasadh arrived. I remembered the last time it had come and how I hardly knew how to pronounce it, much less know what it was. I celebrated it with the Peter and Nasaide's Druid group and invited Jason, giving him a ride. Jason was more involved with Lenore's Green Man Tribe, but he fit in well.

"Have you heard from June, at all?" Nasiade asked me after the ritual. She wore a deep green sun dress with prints of sunflowers scattered about.

"She's moving on, apparently. So should I, right?"

Nasaide ran her hand across my back in apology, but kept silent.

I put the rest of June's belongings in boxes and gave them to Benny and Sam. Sam seemed happy to see me, but kept quiet for the most part, probably feeling guilty about not calling as Benny said. I didn't feel like talking anyway. I was good about not letting the situation affect my job or my interactions with other people, but when it came down to it, I felt as if I was going through the motions. I did what I had to do on automatic programing. But maybe that was okay as a defense mechanism. Maybe all you could do through a difficult time is put one foot in front of the other until it was all over.

My follow up medical appointment for the VA arrived and I went back to the giant building on Irving street. Inside smelled like industrial strength cleaner and the stale musk of people. I'm humbled every time I enter, seeing my fellow vets from wars past. They were proud to have served, sporting their "Vietnam Veteran" caps and sometimes tee shirts that displayed their branch in service.

"What branch were you in?" One gentleman asked me.

"I was in the Navy."

"I figured you were in the Navy. You seem like a Corpsman, am I wrong?"

"No, you're correct. I was a Corpsman."

"It's in the way you walk and the way you hold yourself. You look like a Navy Corpsman."

I took this as a compliment.

My doctor told me that she felt I was improving. She was a younger woman than I imagined a doctor to be, possibly in her mid thirties. She was of Indian descent and spoke with a thick accent. She wore a blue lanyard carrying her ID card.

I told her about June and how she wanted me to move on. She asked how I was handling this.

"Quite well, actually. I haven't had any panic attacks through the ordeal. I've been very focused on remaining stable."

"That's very good to hear," she said, "There is nothing you can do about your ex-girlfriend's decisions, but you can control your reaction. This is a big step for you."

"Yes," I said. "Yes it is."

At the bus stop outside, I ran into Lenore. She was dressed in light blue gown with purple flowers.

"Lenore!" I said.

"Jacob, it's so good to see you!"

"What are you doing here?"

"I'm a veteran," she explained. "Air force."

"I never knew. Wow."

"Yes, I've always been supportive of our military."

"That's great!" My phone rang in my pocket, but I ignored it.

"How are things with you," she asked me.

"They could be better but I'm handling it fine."

"That's too bad. I wish there was something I could do about your situation with June."

I shrugged. "I'll be okay."

We talked about the community and what she wanted from it. Lenore wanted to unite all of the different pagan branches: the Druids, the eclectic Wiccans, the Asatru.

"That would be great. You already seem to have the attention of many of the pagans in the area as an elder."

"That's so sweet of you to say, thank you."

Again, my phone rang in my pocket and again I ignored it. A bus came by but it wasn't mine and Lenore seemed uninterested.

"Which bus are you taking?" I asked her.

"Oh, I'm not taking the bus. Anna is picking me up shortly."

"I see."

For a third time, my phone went off. I answered it.

"It's Benny, listen to me!" Benny's voice rang out frantically.

"I'm listening."

"June is headed to your apartment. She thinks you have a necklace her father gave her."

"But I packed everything…"

"Yes, yes! I have the necklace. I hid it from her!"

"Why would you…?"

"Because I'm a sucker for romance! You are missing the point! June is headed to your place. Get there now!"

"Right!"

I hung up.

"Oh my god!" I said out loud. I stood up from the bus bench and paced. What was I to do? The bus wasn't due for another 15 minutes and it would be slow as hell, stopping every few blocks.

"What's wrong dear? What happened?" Lenore asked me.

"June is headed to my apartment. I don't know how much time I have before she leaves."

"Say no more. Where do we need to take you?" She was waving to the street and I could see Anna driving a blue sedan waving back.

"Jacob needs a ride home. It's very important." Lenore told Anna as she motioned for me to get in the back seat.

"Where are we taking you?" Anna asked.

"Pentagon City," I said. "But I know that's out of your way. If you drop me off at the nearest metro…"

"Nonsense," Lenore interrupted. "We are taking you to Pentagon City."

The traffic was merciless at that hour. It was stop and go all the way down North Capitol Street. Anna seemed nervous as Lenore navigated her through the onslaught of cars, trucks, and buses. We made it down to Rhode Island Avenue, and from Rhode Island we turned on to 14th Street to make a dash for the Interstate 395 Highway.

"We'll get you there. Just keep picturing June waiting for

you." Lenore shouted back at me. The DC streets were loud with horns, street workers, and jaywalkers. We crossed into the mall of monuments and soon were on the highway, avoiding cars seemingly stopped for no reason other than to delay us. Anna swore several times at taxi cabs. She didn't seem to like any of them.

She swerved to the Pentagon exit and soon we were in my neighborhood near the Pentagon City shopping mall.

"You can drop me off right here, please," I said, trying to remain calm, pointing at an opening near the sidewalk. I kissed Lenore on the cheek and thanked her and Anna profusely as I darted from their car to the lobby of my apartment building.

I could feel my heart thumping in my ears. I had chills tingling across my body. I opened my apartment door. It was dark inside, too dark for someone to be visiting.

"Hello?" I called. I could smell her perfume, but it was faint. Nervous, I rushed into the bedroom. It was empty. I checked the guest room and the bathroom. No one was there. I missed her. Maybe it was for the best. Maybe I needed to finally let her go like she told me to.

Defeated, I pulled a chair out from the dining table and sat down. I rubbed my head. She was gone.

"Jacob?" Her voice called out like a ghost in a closet.

Startled, I looked over to the couch in the living room. She sat in her spot in the dark, perfectly still.

"Are you there?" I said, disoriented.

"Yes, I'm here."

I stood up from my seat and approached her, each step feeling heavy. The front door felt too close and too easy to get to, as if she'd run out at any second. But she stayed perfectly still.

"How've you been?" she asked.

"I've been well. I have a job now, in DC."

"That's great."

"Yes."

"How are you?" I asked, but before she could answer I said, "I miss you, June, so damn much."

In the dim blue light I thought I saw her lip quiver. I heard her sniffle. "I..." She started, but she trailed off.

I took a chance and flipped on a light, to see her fully, to see that I wasn't hallucinating. She was real. She was June and she was crying openly now, covering her face with her hands. I sat down slowly beside her, as if she were a frightened bird about to fly away at the slightest sound. I just sat with her, being with her as best as I knew I could. I wanted to kiss her, to hold her, but I wasn't sure what would scare her off.

"I miss you too," she continued. I took another chance and put an arm around her, bringing her into me. She fell limply against my body and continued to cry.

"Then, stay," I said. "Don't leave. Things are different now and stable, I promise."

She nodded, "I know. I believe you."

"I still love you," I said quickly.

"I love you too. I almost left when I realized Benny probably tricked me about the necklace, but being back here with so much you, so much of us, I didn't want to leave."

"Then stay."

"That's what I'm telling you. Take me back."

"Always."

28

June decided she wanted us to move. To be honest I was very happy with our apartment in Virginia, near the shopping mall and with perfect metro access. She wanted to be closer to both of our jobs and so she spent evenings scouring apartment websites and listings in newspapers.

I always seemed to have a problem with the homes she picked out. They were too small or the rent was too high. We both liked the idea of having a guest room, for her because she wanted a place for her mother to sleep when she visited, for me because I wanted a place to practice my witchcraft in privacy. This made the hunt a little more difficult since rent in DC is so ridiculously high.

"Why don't we just stay here?" I asked her.

She scoffed, but gave no response.

I got a text while I was at work one day. June had found a place she was absolutely in love with. She already viewed it and it was perfect for both of us and superbly inexpensive and within our range for rent. She sent pictures but I hardly glanced at them. I was busy that day and decided I would talk to her afterward. She wanted me to meet her at the house in Logan's Circle after work, and I agreed, quickly.

While on the metro, I examined the pictures of the interior that June had sent me. They were pretty dark but I could make out the kitchen, spacious and perfect, and the living room. The house had three rooms and June was quick to remark, "one extra as a guest room and one extra as a den" in her text. I liked the idea, but I was thinking more of converting one into a ritual room. We'd have to talk, of course. I suddenly had a good feeling about this new place, especially after seeing the price. There was something familiar about the pictures too.

I got off on McPherson Square and headed north into Logan. June met me, smiling and giddy in September sun.

"You're going to love it," she said. "It's an older white house up on a hill."

She led me by the hand through the crowd of people getting off work. She seemed to effortlessly glide through them while I was constantly excusing myself and apologizing for bumping into a few folks. Finally, after a turn or two, we were there.

I couldn't believe it when I saw it. Shining as a bright white beacon was the home of Stephen Cook. There was the for rent sign posted outside of the house on the small yard. It looked different in the daytime, even lovely.

"Isn't it perfect?" June said excited beside me.

"Yes," I said absently. How was it possible? Of all the houses to stumble on.

"Have they told you why it was so cheap?" I asked.

She hesitated, "well, they mentioned that someone died in the home, but what does that matter, right? We don't believe in ghosts, do we?"

"Right."

"Do we?"

"Well, what kind of a witch would I be if I couldn't handle a little ghost, right?"

June laughed, "Exactly."

Before long, we were packing, signing papers and collecting keys. We hired movers from a veteran owned and operated moving company. I was relieved to have avoided driving a large rented truck through the curse of DC traffic. The help carrying things up the narrow staircase was also appreciated. Soon we were moved in, and later we were unpacked. This last bit taking much longer with our work schedules. By the end of September, we were successfully settled and there was no sign of Stephen Cook's ghost.

I began to imaging that maybe the sounds Corey and I heard was really just the settling of the house, or the sounds of some trespassing homeless person. That is, until June came to me a few times claiming she saw me in other parts of the house.

"I thought I saw you upstairs in the bedroom," she would say or "I thought I saw the light on in the bathroom."

The final straw came when she came upstairs to my ritual room. I was dusting and rearranging when she walked in, her face was white.

"Jacob, I think our house is haunted," she said.

"What makes you say that?"

"While I was down in the basement doing laundry, I saw someone standing at the doorway. It said my name, Jacob!"

"I'll take care of it," I said and I reached for my ritual dagger on my altar and headed into the bedroom where I had a shoe box with a bundle of sage tucked under the bed. As I lit the sage with an old lighter, I saw him, from the corner of my eye. Stephen Cook was standing by the open closet door in the bedroom, breathing hoarsely, maybe even angrily. His skin was gray and sickly and from what I could make of his hair in that split second, it was wet.

I turned quickly to the closet, holding my athame in one hand, and my lit smudge in the other. There was no one there but the open closet door revealed only blackness inside. As I took a step forward, it began to shut itself. I swore I could see Stephen's cold gray hand gripping the door frame and then disappearing into the darkness before the door closed.